TOO MUCH CRIME ON MY HANDS

MARY FRAME

This book is dedicated to my alpha readers, Mary Baader Kaley and Jennifer Ortiz, who read my words when they are at their worst and still don't hate me.

Mary: you have been my guide from the beginning, and I cannot thank you enough for everything you do. Don't ever leave me. I will find you. Please don't be creeped out by this. . .

Jen: I can't believe I found you on Goodreads. You are the best thing that's ever happened to me on that site. You're probably the best thing that's happened on that site in general, actually.

I love you both! Keep writing!

"I need you to tell me if I'm being haunted."

The gentleman fidgeting on the porch has paper-white hair, baby-blue trousers with yellow suspenders, a white button-up top, and the largest moustache I've ever seen.

The shop typically opens at ten, and it's eight fifteen in the morning. If there's one thing I can say about the people of Castle Cove, it's that they're always interesting.

Today, we're not even opening until noon because I told Tabby I would have brunch with her. There's a sign on the door with all this information.

I have my coffee in hand, ready to ingest a much needed dose of caffeine, but my visitor rushes past me and into the shop.

"Um. *Are* you being haunted?" I ask.

"I'm not sure, that's why I'm here. Can't you tell me?" his voice booms. I don't think he meant to yell at me though.

"That's not really what I do here," I hedge.

"But it's really important." His moustache twitches. He's nervous. Or panicked about something.

I suppose the coffee can wait for a moment. "If your home is attracting negative energies, I might have something to help cleanse the space."

He considers my words for a moment and then nods. "I need something to keep out the dark spirits. Do you have anything for that?"

"Sure." Mournfully, I leave my coffee at the checkout counter and glance out the window into the spring sunshine. May in Castle Cove is warmer than I expected. Even this early in the morning, the fog has already lifted and the bees are buzzing

I lead him over to the herbs and crystals section. We just received a big shipment of them, most with purported healing properties. The inventory has been surprisingly popular with the local residents, not something I really expected from the elderly population of Castle Cove. Though in hindsight, perhaps I should have seen it coming. Just yesterday Mrs. Newsome came in looking for an orange carnelian stone to enhance her love life. I shudder at the thought.

"You could do a simple smudge." I point out a small plastic bag of sage.

His lips tilt downward under the starch-white moustache. "I don't want to smudge anything. I like to keep my house tidy."

"You don't actually—"

"Is that marijuana?" He peers closer at the bag.

"No, it's sage."

"Do you inhale it?"

"No. You light it on fire and then you let the smoke cleanse the area of impurities." According to the instructions on the bag, anyway.

"It might not be ghosts in my house. It might be the little people. Do you have anything for that?"

"Little people?"

"Yes," he rumbles. "They snuck into my house and-and did things!"

Now I'm curious. "What kind of things?"

A strange beeping at the front counter distracts me. It sounds like a cell phone ringing, the tone melodic and muffled.

"Why don't you take a look at the various herbal packages I have here, Mr., uh . . ."

"Mr. Godfrey."

"Right. Mr. Godfrey. There may be some other items you can use. Just check out the instructions on the bag. I'll be back in a moment."

The noise gets louder as I approach the front counter. I search the drawers for the source.

It's the old burner phone. I forgot about it since there's no reception here. I pick it up and stare at the screen. There's one single bar of service and the little infinity-like symbol indicating a voicemail.

It's probably just a telemarketer or a wrong number, but I press the voicemail key anyway.

You have one new message, the robotic tone tells me. Then the call clicks on. At first, I don't hear anything. There's a bit of shuffling and wind, and I start to think someone butt-dialed the number.

But then I hear the voice. A male voice, roughened with time, too many cigarettes and a general disdain of humanity.

"I don't give a flying—" The call cuts out.

It's only five words, but even with the wind in the background, I would recognize that voice saying that phrase anywhere. It's the same voice from my nightmares.

"Excuse me, miss." Mr. Godfrey is at the counter with his hands full of packages. "Can I get a bulk discount?"

I nod, my brain jumping in a million directions, and ring him up on autopilot. I'm not sure exactly how much I charge him but he hands me cash and leaves.

He might have said something else, or asked me something else, but if he did I didn't hear it over the buzzing in my head.

Our parents found the number to the burner phone. But how?

I take a deep breath and sink to the floor, my back to the wall.

They've never been the type to let go of what they consider theirs. And I'm sure they're pissed about how we left and what we took.

We've been in Castle Cove now for two months. I was beginning to get comfortable. First mistake.

Will we be on the move forever? Will they ever give up trying to find us?

But maybe they haven't actually found us, just because they have the burner number. I purchased the phone in another state. The area code is from the other side of the country. Maybe they have the number but not our physical location.

We have to do *something* though.

A loud rapping at the door jerks me from my thoughts.

Gathering my wits about me, I get up and answer it.

"Troy." My voice is a little crisp from the flash of anxiety.

"Ruby." He matches my formal tone. He's wearing his police uniform. I haven't seen him in almost a week, since the last dinner at his sister Tabby's house. Tabby and I have become fast friends, something I never thought I would have. Second mistake.

Getting too close. Having too much to lose.

Jared was not present, thankfully. I haven't talked to him since . . .

I don't want to think about that now.

I force myself to relax. *Get a grip lady.*

Stepping back, I let him into the shop. I turn around and straighten something on a shelf that doesn't need adjusting, buying time to calm my nerves and shrug into my Ruby mindset.

"What brings you to this side of the neighborhood so early?" I ask before turning back around to face him.

"Well," he pulls off his hat and scrubs a hand through his hair, "I need to talk to you about a case."

"Oh, no. No more cases for me."

"Hold on now, let me finish. We've been having some strange occurrences throughout town."

"Yeah?"

"We're not sure exactly what it is. People are reporting things moved around their houses. Odd things, like spoons being put in purses and toilet brushes in the fridge. There's already been four incidents so far."

My brows rise. "Have you found any little people?"

His lips purse. "I can see Mr. Godfrey has been here."

"You just missed him."

"Darn." He snaps his fingers. "He's only been calling me every two hours to check on the status of the case. I was starting to miss talking to the guy."

"I could call him back for you."

"If you do that I will be forced to use my cuffs on you, and not in the fun way."

I laugh, my earlier worries fading a bit with the banter.

Troy grins before continuing. "The weirdest thing is that nothing is missing from these break-ins, so people are starting to suspect the culprit is more . . . supernatural in nature. And, well, you are the resident mystic." His grin tilts into a lopsided smile.

"Right." Lucky me. Most of what I know about the supernatural comes from a TV show. But I don't think Sam and Dean are going to jump in and save me from this conversation. "I really wish I could help you."

His face brightens. "Then you can."

"No. I really can't. I'm sorry, Troy. You and . . ." I stall out before I can say his name, the last time I saw Jared flashing through my mind. I clear my throat. "You and Jared are smart. You'll figure it out eventually. You don't need me."

He grimaces. "That's not true, Ruby. This might really be some kind of haunting or something."

"That killed you, didn't it?"

"A little, on the inside, but even I have to admit there's something weird happening around here."

"I'm sorry, but even if I did think it was ghosts, that's not really what I do. It's not going to happen."

"All right then. I had to at least try." He pauses at the door, placing his hat back on his head. "If you change your mind, will you let me know?"

"Absolutely."

He opens the door and my mouth opens before I can stop myself.

"Are you going to Ben's tonight for trivia, or are you on duty?"

A trick question to see if Jared is working tonight, or if he'll be at Ben's, too.

I shouldn't be thinking about him. I have bigger things to worry about. I'm still reeling from the unexpected phone call. I know it might not mean anything, but what if it does? I *should* stay home, tell Paige what's going on, maybe even think about leaving town.

But I want to see him . . . talk to him, just one more time.

"Anderson is on duty tonight." Troy falls neatly into my trap. "Are you going?"

If Anderson is on patrol tonight, Jared has the night off.

I nod. "Yeah. I'll see you then."

2

————

$\mathcal{A}$fter Troy leaves, I pick up my cooling coffee and make my way out to the porch.

I'm glad he showed up when he did to distract me from the panic and force me to put my thoughts in order. If the parents are on our tail, panic will be as helpful as a stick in the eye.

Mr. Bingel is occupying his usual spot this time every day: on his knees, trimming his roses, with a wide-brimmed hat and bright-yellow gardening gloves. Next to him are two little people—and not the kind Mr. Godfrey is worried about—kneeling, copying his pose in matching hats and gloves.

"Good morning, Miss Ruby!" Gary waves at me frantically when I venture out to the porch swing.

"Good morning, boys," I return, injecting brightness into my tone.

Mr. Bingel gives me a dirty look and says something to Gary to get him to turn back around.

Some things don't change.

The boys have, however, and their transformation is pretty incredible. They've both put on some weight and are consistently happy and clean.

Their father still hasn't turned up. I heard from Tabby who heard from Troy who heard from Jared that they think he left the country.

I wish my parents would abandon me.

I couldn't hear the news from Jared himself because, well, I haven't seen Jared since the night the boys came home with Mr. Bingel. And yet, I still come out here every morning by eight thirty, expecting . . . I don't know what. He probably thinks I'm crazy. I think I'm crazy. So why am I still sitting out here?

It doesn't matter. I don't want to see him. So why am I going to trivia tonight?

And with that thought, he comes running around the corner in athletic shorts and a tank top, butt flexing with every stride.

Okay, that's why.

Until the night that changed everything, Jared used to run by my place every morning without a glance. But since that fateful night, I haven't seen him. Today, he surprises me.

"Good morning," he calls with a wave.

My hand lifts. "Goo—"

"Good morning, Deputy!" Mr. Bingel calls. The boys are waving excitedly, their little gloved hands flapping as Jared runs past.

My hand drops back to my lap.

He nods at them and then his eyes flick in my direction before he disappears from view. Not nearly long enough to get any idea of what he's thinking.

I don't blame him if he's mad at me. I'm mad at me.

Not that it matters. We won't be here much longer anyway, which is one of the reasons I pushed him away. After I totally led him on and invited him in.

My cheeks flush, remembering.

"Did you want to come in?" I asked him that night.

He stared at me, his gaze as intense as ever. I flushed under the weight of his scrutiny.

Then he stepped over the threshold.

It wasn't like before, in the laundry room, when I had thrown myself at him and wrapped around him like an anaconda.

No, it was much, much worse.

He came at me carefully, taking his time, making my heart race faster in stark contrast to his own languid movements. His hands slid around my jaw and cupped my face. He watched me for a few, long seconds, his eyes searching my face for something important. His lips were sweet when they met mine with a slow and sure purpose.

One hand glided down my back and the other cupped the back of my head, angling me closer.

We made out in the doorway for a long time, his hands on my waist and my hands in his hair. He kissed me like he meant it.

And then I freaked.

It was too much. Too good. If we kept going, if I let him in, it wouldn't be a one-and-done deal.

He felt like forever.

I didn't have forever.

What I had was a child to raise. Not only were we leaving, I couldn't risk letting anyone into my life. I couldn't risk getting close to anyone and having them figure out the truth. I had to protect Paige at any cost. My wants were unimportant.

I pushed him away. "You need to leave."

His eyes were wide with confusion, concern, hurt. "Are you oka—"

"Go." We were right next to the door, making it almost too easy to shove him out and lock the door with a loud click. I stood there with my forehead against the hard wood, wondering what was wrong with me.

Conflicting emotions warred inside of me. I wanted him, I couldn't have him, I needed him, and he needed . . . not me. Anything but me.

He didn't argue. He didn't fight me. He left.

I haven't seen him since.

Until today.

"You have to come with me to book club next weekend," Tabby informs me over waffles at the country club an hour later. "It's the first monthly meeting in like forever."

I've never eaten at the country club, but apparently Ben—who is still not Tabby's boyfriend—runs the bar for special events like weddings and such. He gave her a free voucher for the brunch, which she decided to share with me. I agreed to go with her last week. I should have bailed. Spending time with her is like digging the knife of regret in a little deeper, especially after my wake-up call this morning. But she didn't give me a choice. She came and got me and now we're here, sitting at a white-linen-covered table, being waited on by elegantly dressed staff, and surrounded by well-dressed people who probably have names like Evangeline and Linus. There's a freshly snipped red rose in an elegant vase on the table between us, and it reminds me of my parents.

I focus on the conversation at hand. I do not want to go back there.

"Book club?" I spear a strawberry with my fork. "I didn't know there was a book club."

"It's not always active." She shrugs and takes a large gulp of orange juice. "It keeps disbanding and then reforming."

"Do I want to know why?" If there's one thing I've learned since moving to Castle Cove, it's to expect the unexpected.

"They keep disagreeing over what we're telling people we're reading."

I have to repeat the sentence in my head for it to make sense. "Wait, what you're *telling* people you're reading? Not what you're *actually* reading?"

She nods. "You see, we have to seem legit. So we tell people we're reading, you know, works of literary genius like *War and Peace*, or *The Martian*, but really we're reading something completely different."

"What's this month's book?"

She leans forward a little and lowers her voice, glancing around before delivering the title like it's a state secret or something.

"*Lanie's Choice*," she whispers.

"What's it about? Is that like *Sophie's Choice*? I haven't heard of it."

"No, nothing like *Sophie's Choice*. It's uh . . . it's about a girl named Lanie." She squirms a little in her seat, picking at her waffle with her fork and not making eye contact. "And she has to make a choice." Her voice is strangled.

"Why are you being weird? What kind of choice?"

"Between . . . you know." Her hand flaps at me. Is she blushing? "Some hot aliens or something." The last words are muffled.

I laugh. "What?"

"It's alien porn, okay? She has to choose between all these hot aliens with horns and giant dicks." Her voice gets louder as she speaks, and the word "dick" comes out full volume.

The couple at the table next to us, in white polo shirts and expensive haircuts, shoots us withering looks.

"Mrs. Olsen wants to read that?" I ask.

"*Wants* to read that? She insists. There would be no book club if it weren't full of smut. Last month it was were-dragons."

Just when you think you've heard it all. "I didn't even know that was a thing."

"Well it is. It was pretty hot. So are you in?"

"What are we pretending to read this month?"

"*Northanger Abbey.* That's the reason we disbanded last month. Mrs. Hale wanted to pretend to read *Pride and Prejudice.*" She nods like this makes so much sense.

"This sounds really fantastic. How many of the old biddies will be there?"

"Most of them. It's either amusing or frightening, depending on their moods."

I laugh and take a sip of my orange juice.

I really am going to miss this crazy town. I wonder if wherever Paige and I end up next will be half as entertaining. I wonder if there will be a Tabby, someone who forces their friendship on me like a rabid dog, or a goofball like Troy, or a Jared.

The rose on the table catches my eye again. My parents. They're always there, between me and everything I want. They always got me a gift for my birthday, not because they actually cared, but so when they asked me to do stuff for them, they could use it as a reminder of how good they were to me. Their gifts were always passive-aggressive, like a super-expensive, brand-name shirt that was four sizes too small. And they always came with one more thing—a single red rose.

It was weird. I still don't understand the rose. Maybe so every time I saw one, I would think of them.

It's obviously working.

"Earth to Ruby." Tabby snaps her fingers in my face.

"Oh, sorry."

"Did you have a vision?" she asks, her voice awed.

"Sort of."

"Was it anything good? Are we going to win the lotto?"

"No, nothing good."

She makes a face. "Something bad?"

"It was nothing." Time for a subject change, something guaranteed to divert her attention. "What's going on with you and Ben?"

She impales a piece of melon on her plate with her fork, the metal utensil knocking the fine china forward a couple inches. "Nothing." She shoves the offending fruit in her mouth.

"Nothing at all?"

She doesn't answer, pointing to her mouth to indicate she's chewing, her jaw moving up and down as if the poor little piece of melon is actually the world's largest piece of taffy or something.

"You can't avoid the question forever."

She swallows. "Watch me. What are you doing after this?"

"Following you around until you tell me the story with Ben."

"There is no story. There will never be a story. Hence the frustration. If we're going to talk about this, then we're also going to talk about Jared."

I hold up my hands. "You win."

She grins. "You're so easy."

"Don't tell Mrs. Olsen."

She laughs. "So really, what happened with you and Jared? He's been all mopey and weirder than normal."

Thinking about it makes me flush with embarrassment. He obviously thinks I'm insane. Hell, I think I'm insane.

I shove the shame away. It's for the best, really. It won't matter soon. We'll be gone and he'll move on. The thought makes my heart heavy.

"Nothing happened," I say. "We're friends."

"Yeah, right. So are Ben and I."

"And I totally believe you." I inject my voice with sickly sweet sincerity.

She laughs. "You super suck."

3

At one, I head to Paige's school for the parent-teacher conference.

Castle Cove Elementary is the smallest school I've ever seen, even though it goes from kindergarten to eighth grade. Each grade has its own small room. Then there's the office, the music room, and that's about it. The grounds have one basketball court, one swing set, and a grassy yard.

It's more intimate than what I grew up with, the few times I was allowed to go to school.

I meet Paige's teacher in one of the classrooms. Watercolor paintings are taped up on one wall and a periodic table on another. The teacher's desk is cluttered with papers, supplies, and a coffee mug that reads *I'm a Grandma, What's Your Superpower?*

"Paige is a wonderful, bright student. Curious about everything," Mrs. Downey tells me. She's got to be at least a hundred years old. She has more wrinkles than a shar-pei and probably weighs less than a hundred pounds. But her eyes are kind and sharp underneath her thick glasses.

Paige has Mrs. Downey for most of her classes, but they have separate instructors for art and music.

"She's too smart sometimes," I say.

"She's adapted very well. She always behaves and doesn't have a bad word to say about anyone. It's obvious she enjoys school and she contributes regularly."

I'm a little surprised at that last bit. The parents drilled into us the importance of being inconspicuous. Never attract attention, never be memorable, yet here Paige is "contributing regularly." Of course she's going to spread her wings and shake off our parents' teachings more and more. That's a good thing. At least, that's what I tell myself. This is an ideal place to raise Paige. The school and the town itself feel more like an extended family than a physical location.

And yet we can't stay.

Will she "contribute regularly" at the next place we end up?

After the conference, I wait for Paige to finish her last class of the day so I can walk home with her.

"We have to talk," I say once we've left the schoolyard behind and moved past all the waiting busses and children.

"About what?" She shrugs her backpack up higher on her shoulders and turns her face in my direction.

I hesitate. I need to tell her about the phone call. But I don't want to freak her out, and I don't want to say their names, as if doing so will conjure them quicker.

They who shall not be named.

"Paige." I take a quick breath. "I . . . got a call on the burner phone. A voicemail. It was Father."

She halts in the middle of the sidewalk and I stop next to her. We're under the shade of a large tree in a residential area, her face dappled by the sun shining through the leaves.

I glance around quickly, but no one is around or close enough to hear our conversation.

"What did he say?" Her voice hitches on the last word.

"He didn't really say anything, it was more like he was talking to someone else when the voicemail clicked on and then he hung up mid-sentence."

Her gaze focuses on the ground between us. "What does this mean?"

"I'm not sure yet. We knew they would look for us. They may have found our old phone number, but it doesn't necessarily mean they've found us." I try to reassure her, but the words don't erase the fear clouding her eyes.

"What are we going to do?"

"I'm not sure yet. But I'll think of something. Don't worry, I promise I'll take care of you."

She nods and we keep walking in silence, each lost in our own thoughts.

I hope I can keep my promise.

My whole life has been spent either doing whatever my parents told me or taking care of Paige. I didn't really have a purpose until she was born, at which point I, too, was just a kid. Sometime over the years she became my sole focus. I hope I'll find a way to make my promise come true. I'm afraid I won't be able to.

The whole reason we left—finally, and without enough money—was my fault. I had to protect her.

The job was simple, but big, the biggest I had been involved in so far. We were working a con on an old, rich guy. I'd gotten hired as one of his many maids. We often targeted the wealthy, but this guy was insanely rich. The house was large enough to require a staff the size of a small hotel's. And he was eccentric. Every corner of the house had to be shiny clean. If there was even a speck of dust left on a shelf, the house manager would be on your ass.

It was difficult to maintain both the actual job and the job my parents had assigned to me. My task was to scope the place out for anything of value—of which there was a lot—and then sneak Paige in to take the items when the rest of the house was occupied with staff meetings and such—which we had every other week.

Our parents had a fence to sell the items overseas, and then they'd have the balance transferred into an offshore account. It was more than that, though. They also had a guy to make duplicates of antique pieces.

They could sell the same "priceless" antiques many times over to unsuspecting buyers. It was one of their favorite routines.

They kept a lot of their business hush-hush from me, but Paige is sneaky as a mouse when she wants to be. And she has ears like a bat.

I snuck her into the old guy's house right before the staff meeting. I barely paid attention while the house manager droned on and on about keeping our uniforms impeccable—even though our job was to clean—and being inconspicuous and quiet and everywhere at once. During the meeting, my eyes flicked to the clock constantly. We had timed her mission multiple times. I had walked the halls, noting how long it took to get from one floor to the other. We'd mapped the most efficient route, gaps in security-camera coverage, places to hide if needed, everything. But on that day, right when I imagined Paige was probably in the owner's bedroom grabbing some diamond cufflinks, the meeting ended early. Someone pulled the fire alarm.

I couldn't warn her. It was the most stressful thirty minutes of my life from when the meeting ended until I could confirm Paige had exited the house without getting caught.

That night, our parents pulled me into the study. The room was decked in tall shelving with books they would never read, gleaming wood inlays they couldn't afford, and a large mahogany desk straight out of a PBS period drama. Not that they ever watched PBS.

"Since Paige's attempt failed, we want to try something else," Mother said, sitting on the edge of the large desk while Father sat in the plush leather chair on the other side.

"What else?" I asked, already wary of their response.

"The old guy. He likes you," she said.

The old guy was Wallace Jackson. His family had made their money in oil a hundred years ago and then invested wisely. He was a widower and almost seventy.

"I guess," I said, shrugging my shoulders.

They exchanged a glance and then Father spoke. "We've had people watching him, and they've seen the way he looks at you."

"You've been spying on me?"

"Not you, Wallace," Mother clarified. "They said he flirts with you. Is that true?"

"No, it's not true. He's nice to everyone. This is ridiculous." My anger rose. They wanted to whore me out to some old guy? I guess I should have known better than to put anything past them, but they'd never done *this* before. "You know those types of cons only work in the movies. He's not going to marry me without a prenup and the odds of gaining anything more than some jewelry is slim."

"Well," Mother shrugged one slim shoulder, "since Paige failed, we have to try something. Otherwise, we've wasted all this time. We don't need you to marry him, just seduce him. Think of the time you'll spend with him. It will give us the opportunity to find his weaknesses. He might give you gifts or even take you to his chateau in France. It's not a big deal. You should be so lucky to get an old guy near the end. It's perfect."

"I don't think we need to do this. Paige didn't fail. No one caught her."

"You're right," Father said. "And since she did manage to get the Ming vase and the Japanese lacquer box, they'll be more suspicious. You won't be able to sneak her in again. We need a new plan."

"I'm not sleeping with Wallace." I couldn't even believe they would suggest it. They knew that the cops—and Wallace's own security staff—would be looking for someone suspicious on the inside, and since the fake background check they'd provided me was, well, fake, it was only a matter of time until I was put in the spotlight.

They exchanged another glance.

Mother smiled at me, more a baring of the teeth than anything reassuring. "Fine. Since we're running out of funds to maintain your lifestyle, and you refuse to do your part, we'll have to use Paige for something else instead."

My heart dropped into my stomach. "What do you mean?"

"If you won't contribute to our household, I'm sure we can find a use for your sister."

They wouldn't . . .

There was a time, not quite a year ago, they'd had some friends over for dinner. Three men, all impeccably dressed. The leader of the group—obvious from the way Mother had preened all over him—had been an older guy, some big-shot attorney. The parents had made Paige serve drinks in the study after dinner and she'd told me the guy had looked at her funny. Made her feel weird. She'd heard them talking about girls, the guy ran some kind of business on the side, but she hadn't understand what they were talking about.

But I had.

My parents were always trying to find influential friends to further their own agendas, but I'd never thought they would get into *that* kind of business. They'd used Paige's happiness against me before, even sending her away once to mess with my head, but they'd always talked about her like she was their golden ticket, whereas mine was distinctly brass at best.

"What are you going to make her do?"

"What do you care? You won't have to do it. Isn't that what you care about most? Yourself?" Her voice was bitter and accusatory.

I should have seen it coming. This was what it always came down to. They used my love of Paige against me. They knew I would do anything for her.

"Fine," I said. "I'll seduce Wallace."

My dad patted my hand, like I had agreed to babysit or take out the trash instead of screwing an old man. Both literally and figuratively. "That's a good girl."

I left his office knowing one thing for sure: we had to leave. Their requests would only get more outlandish and demanding, and even if I did what they asked, they would still use Paige to show me who was in control.

They'd used her to manipulate me before, but actually *using* her? If they tried to use her for . . . no, they wouldn't. They couldn't. She was too young.

But deep down, I knew better.

They would sell their own daughter if it got them what they wanted.

Paige and I had been saving money whenever we could, but it wasn't happening fast enough. We could only hide a few hundred dollars at a time. But it didn't matter anymore. I would rather starve on the streets than live with them for another moment.

I talked to Paige that night and we agreed to leave. No more waiting for the right time that would never come. After the parents were asleep, I used the computer in the study to hack into their Cayman Islands accounts. I transferred the money to a local bank in my name. It wasn't a lot—a few thousand, enough to buy a cheap car and get us on the road. However, the only way I could get the money to transfer quickly required a hack that set off some alarms and locked the account. It didn't matter. We were gone before the parents realized what we had done.

We walked into town and waited outside all night until the bank opened. I withdrew the money and immediately closed the account. Then we went to a local used-car dealer and paid cash for the car. Then we were free.

But are we still?

4

Paige didn't want to talk when I got home. She went straight to her room, shut the door, and only emerged to ask if she could spend the night at Naomi's.

I couldn't deny her request. We don't have much longer to spend in Castle Cove. We always knew we would have to leave, eventually, before Ruby returned, but we both thought we would have more time.

With our parents searching for us, maybe even on our trail, who knows how much time we really have? We can't live in ignorant bliss any longer.

I'm grateful when Tabby shows up to take me to trivia night, anything to stop thinking about all the things that could happen. All the things that *will* happen.

Friday night at Ben's is always the same. Wall to wall people, Tabby sneaking behind the bar stealing drinks, and the Newsomes getting into a fight.

But it's not the same. Everyone here, from the old drunk sitting at the corner of the bar sleeping, to the men playing at the pool table, and Tabby sneaking behind the bar as soon as Ben goes to boot the Newsomes . . . they'll all be here next week and next month and next year.

I won't.

"Come back when you can behave like adults!" Ben yells out the door. His words barely register over the buzz of the crowd.

"That's never going to happen." Tabby laughs. "This time they didn't even make it to eight o'clock. Here, drink this." She shoves a glass in my hand.

I mentally shrug off the melancholy that's wrapped itself around my mind like a python. I don't have forever here, not like everyone else, but what I do have I want to enjoy.

My brows lift at the glass. "What's this one?"

She shrugs. "Oh, you know, some roofies, rat poison, the usual."

"Sounds delicious."

Tabby always has the uncanny ability to make light of everything, to make me laugh no matter what else is going on in my life. Out of everyone in Castle Cove, I think I'm going to miss her the most.

The trivia thing is about to start. I'm not sure how it all works, but I'm sure someone will explain it eventually.

"Hello, ladies." Troy slides into the booth across from me and Tabby.

She immediately pushes a glass in his direction.

He grimaces at the purple-colored concoction. "What is this foo-foo crap?"

"Oh please, you drink this all the time at my house when I give you pedicures."

Troy glances around with a pained expression. "Keep your voice down," he begs.

Tabby laughs.

After another darting glance around the room, Troy takes the shot.

Tabby whoops and then her attention is on me. "Your turn."

I take the shot, much slower than Troy, and put the glass on the table next to his.

Tabby claps. "Now we're ready for trivia."

"How does this work, anyway?" I ask.

"Ben hands out one blank paper for each group to write our answers on. He'll call out the questions, and we answer as a group. Once all the questions are over, we turn in our answers for grading. Oh, we need a group name. I think we should call ourselves . . ." She taps her finger on her pursed lips while she thinks.

"The youngest people in the room," Troy offers.

"No."

"The only people who haven't had knee or hip surgery."

"No, Troy." She smacks him in the arm. "It has to be trivia related."

"Quiz in my pants."

She makes a face. "Gross."

"Trivia Newton John."

We laugh.

"That is clever," I say.

"Then it's set." Troy claps his hands once. "Where's the rest of our team?"

"More than just us?" Tabby asks. I steel myself. After all, I know the answer already.

"Yeah, Jared and Eleanor are coming."

My stomach immediately drops to my toes. I haven't seen Jared, well, since he ran by this morning, but . . . Jared and *Eleanor*?

"They're coming together?" I fidget with the drink napkin on the table in front of me. All of Ben's napkins have an imprint of a frog with a crown on its head. They match the fake frogs hanging from the ceiling over the bar. I rub the ridge in the napkin with my thumb, suddenly super interested in the stupid frog's head.

Troy shrugs but eyes me over the rim of his glass before he takes a sip. "Yeah. That's not a problem, right, since you and Jared are just friends?"

"Right. No problem. Totally."

"Speak of the devil." Troy stands to greet Jared and Eleanor.

I can't quite make myself look at them. Instead, I keep my gaze riveted on the napkin in my hands.

"You guys made it," Tabby says. "I didn't know you were bringing *Eleanor*. What in the world took you so long? Did you guys get distracted on the way here?" she asks a bit too loudly.

That makes me look up in time to see Tabby winking

in my direction.

She's totally full of it, but the thought still makes me a little queasy.

Jared lifts a brow. "You told me to be here around—"

Tabby elbows him in the side. "Oh, hey, look, Ben's passing out the answer sheets."

Now that I've looked up, I can't look away. Jared is wearing jeans and a T-shirt. All very normal and nothing to gawk over, but it doesn't stop me from staring. He hasn't shaved in a couple of days but the stubble on his chin doesn't conceal his strong jawline. He smiles at me, but the movement doesn't reach his eyes.

Jared and Eleanor get in the circular booth with us. Somehow, I end up at the top of the curve next to Jared. I'm blocked in by Tabby on one side, and on my other side is Jared, Eleanor, then Troy.

I smile and say hi to our new teammates and force myself to act normal.

Ben reaches our table and passes a paper to Tabby. "Put your group name at the top."

"Yeah, yeah, I know." She snatches the pen from him.

He looks like he wants to say something else but then shakes his head and turns toward the next group.

"What's the theme tonight?" Jared asks.

"I think it's the 1950s," Tabby says.

Troy scoffs. "Ugh, old people trivia. Again."

"Gotta cater to the crowd," Jared says.

"Speak for yourself old man."

"You're a year younger than me."

"Try three years and three times as manly." Troy

puffs out his chest, making us laugh, and then he winks at Eleanor.

She blushes.

"Try a year and a half and twice as ridiculous," Jared says.

"You're both ridiculous," Tabby says. "And you're both old men."

"Tabby, we have the same birthday," Troy says.

"You're at least a few minutes older and I look way younger."

Jared nods, brimming with sincerity. "She does look younger than you."

"Don't make me come over there." Troy reaches around Eleanor, trying to get to Jared. She squeaks and tries to move out of the way, but Troy's undeterred, his hands grabbing at Jared.

"Boys, stop." Tabby stretches across the table and smacks her brother upside the head. "You're being ridiculous."

"You're calling us ridiculous?" Troy's eyebrows lift. "Pot. Kettle. Black."

The insults stop when Ben gets on the stage and steps up to the microphone. "Some quick rules." His voice echoes over the bar.

The crowd quiets down.

Except for one person.

"Boo," Tabby yells.

Ben shields his eyes from the glare of the stage lights. "Tabby, settle down."

"I'll settle down your face," she calls back.

A few chuckles titter around the room.

"Did you mean that to sound like a sex thing? Because it sounded like a sex thing," Troy says with a grimace.

"It was supposed to sound tough." She wrinkles her nose. "I am off my game tonight."

"Rule number one," Ben continues, undeterred. "No sharing answers with other groups."

"Duh," Tabby says.

"Rule number two, no switching groups. Whoever you're sitting with now is who you're stuck with. Rule number three, no sore losers. That's for you, Tabby."

"I resent that!" she yells, and then in a lower voice, "What makes him think I would lose?"

"Have you ever won?" Troy asks.

"So? Wouldn't that make a win more likely? Law of averages and all?"

"We'll start out with some easy questions," Ben's voice booms over the microphone. "Number one: What teen idol sang 'Kookie, Kookie [Lend Me Your Comb]'?"

"What the hell is that shit?" Tabby says. "This is supposed to be easy?"

"Anyone have any ideas?" Troy asks.

"Isn't it the guy from *77 Sunset Strip*?" I whisper, leaning in.

Eyes swing toward me.

"What is that?" Tabby asks.

"It's a TV show from the fifties," I say. "You know, he was always combing his hair."

"No, I don't know. How the hell do you know about

some random TV show from the 1950s?" Tabby asks.

"Paige and I watch a lot of old shows. It's sort of a thing we do."

"Dude. Yes. That's amazing. We will smoke this trivia night." Tabby holds her hand up for a high five and I smack it.

"I still don't know the guy's name," I say.

"It's okay, I'm going to put 'dude from 77 Sunset Strip.' That has to be a valid answer because it's the worst question ever."

Ben moves on to the next question. "Which hugely popular trilogy was awarded the International Fantasy Award in 1957?"

Tabby looks at me and I shrug. "I got nothing."

No one else speaks for a moment.

"It's *The Lord of the Rings*," Eleanor says so quietly I almost don't hear her.

"What?" Tabby barks.

"*The Lord of the Rings*," Troy repeats for her, louder. "Geez, Tabby, I'm going to start calling you Miss Viola."

"Defensive much?" Tabby says to Troy and then to Eleanor, "Nice work." She scribbles down the answer.

I think it's the first time Eleanor has said anything all night. I almost forgot she was here.

Ben rattles off a few more questions, of which I know nothing, but between the five of us we attempt to answer most of them.

"Which 1950s TV show started October 15, 1951, and ran until May 6, 1957?"

I immediately lean in. "*I Love Lucy*."

Tabby starts writing the answer down, but then Jared bends in my direction, his leg pressing against mine. "*The Roy Rogers Show* was on during the same time."

I turn my head toward him. "Yeah but Roy Rogers is no Lucille Ball."

He smiles slowly, his eyes lighting up with the motion. "That's true."

I smile back at him. Our eyes lock and hold. A flash of memory assaults me, his lips on mine—not the passionate embrace when I practically attacked him, but the soft movement of his mouth on mine when he kissed me like my lips were something to be revered. His gaze flicks to my mouth and I wonder if he's remembering the same thing.

"We're agreed on *I Love Lucy* then?" Tabby confirms, breaking the spell.

"Uh, yeah," Jared says.

I can't look back at Jared. I glance around the table. Tabby is scribbling on the paper in front of her and Troy is making faces at Eleanor, trying to make her laugh.

Ben continues calling out questions at intervals. Other than the TV show questions, I can't contribute much, but it is fun between Tabby getting all competitive and Troy and Jared trying to insult each other.

The whole thing takes less than an hour, and when all the questions have been read, Ben comes back around to pick up the answer sheets.

"Tabby, it's time to put the pencil down, you know the rules," he says, since Tabby is still furiously erasing and scribbling things down.

"Shhh." She takes a moment from her writing to press a finger to his lips, smooshing them down and to the side. "Just let it happen."

When she removes her finger, he grabs the paper from her hand.

"Hey!"

"Ben, are we still on for the pool tournament on Thursday?" Troy interrupts.

"Can't. Thursday night is mocktail party night at the senior center."

"Mocktail party?" I ask.

Ben explains, "Most of the old folks there can't drink because it interferes with their meds, so we started a thing last month. Mocktails: fake cocktails. They get dressed up and pretend they're drinking cosmos but it's really cranberry juice and soda water."

"Sounds like a good time." Tabby fakes a gag.

"Maybe too much of a good time. There's no booze, but they like to act like they're hammered. I caught Mrs. Hale and Mr. Godfrey trying to steal a package of the little umbrellas I put in the drinks."

"What were they going to do with those?" Jared asks.

"You know, I don't want to know."

Another group calls Ben over and he leaves. Tabby explains to me how he'll review and tally the answers and decide who won.

"What does the winner get?" Eleanor asks.

"The trophy." Tabby nods in the direction of the bar.

"That's a trophy?" Eleanor's voice is a little strangled.

The item in question is resting at the end of the bar,

all by itself in the center of the gleaming wood. It's a red-and-white beer can with a variety of objects glued to it, from little green GI Joes to a plastic banana.

"And you want to win this so bad because . . ." Troy asks Tabby.

"You know I like to win, I don't care if the prize is a piece of junk. I want it."

Eleanor and Jared start having a discussion about a charity event at the library involving local law enforcement while Tabby and Troy argue about who won the last trivia night.

I watch them all. Listening, but not really engaging. Tabby and Troy are sitting across from each other, so Tabby is leaning forward, getting irritated with her brother.

Jared is resting his arms on the table, but facing Eleanor. Eleanor is focused completely on him as he talks, her hands clenched in her lap.

Is talking to him making her nervous? I remember what it's like to have his intense gaze focused on you like you're the only person in the room.

I can't help but wonder, if they arrived together, will they be leaving together? I might have to get out of here before I can find out. Even though it's obvious to me they aren't together like that, despite what Tabby tried to insinuate earlier, it doesn't mean something won't happen between them. Something could start for them tonight, even. With a sinking in my gut, I realize I really don't want to know.

After a few minutes, Ben is back on the mic. He reads

out the questions again, along with the correct answers—I was right about *I Love Lucy*—before he announces the winner. We lost by two questions.

"I demand a recount!" Tabby yells.

"We don't do recounts, Tabby, sit down," Ben says over the microphone.

The group who won, Agatha Quiztie, cheers and claps, and the rest of the room groans.

Once they've collected their trophy, people shuffle around the bar as some pack up to leave or move over to the pool tables and dartboards.

Tabby and Ben decide to play a game of pool; I don't want to hang around.

"I think I'm going to head home," I tell Tabby. "You can stay. I'll walk," I assure her when she starts to put down her pool cue.

"I'm leaving, too," Troy says. "I'm taking Eleanor home. I can drop you off on the way if you want."

"I can take you, Ruby," Jared interrupts. "You're on my way and that way Troy doesn't have to double back after he drops off Eleanor."

My stomach does a mini somersault. Alone with Jared in a car the entire way home? That sounds like a terrible idea. But it would be weirder to object. Plus, even though I know I'm no good for him and I won't be here much longer anyway, some sick little part of me craves his presence.

"Sounds good," I agree.

Troy nods at him and we all make our way toward the exit.

I follow Troy out. He pulls his keys out of his back pocket and a small rectangular shape falls out onto the floor.

I bend over to retrieve it. "Troy. You dropped this . . . ketchup?" I frown in confusion.

An individual-sized ketchup packet was in his pocket, like the kind you get at a fast food restaurant. There aren't any fast food restaurants around here though. And also, why does he have ketchup in his pocket?

"Oh, thanks." He grins and takes it from me, shoving it back in his pants without explanation and continuing toward the door.

Weird, but whatever.

We say our goodbyes in the parking lot before Troy and Eleanor head out.

Jared opens the door to his Jeep for me.

"Thank you for taking me home," I say when we're driving down the dark road.

"It's no problem."

"So . . . how have you been?" Okay, lamest fishing-for-information attempt that's ever come out of my mouth.

He knows it too, if the slight uptick at the corner of his mouth is any indication. "I've been fine."

"Listen, I'm sorry about—"

"You don't need to apologize to me, Ruby."

"I know I don't need to. I want to. It was rude of me to . . ." Lead you on and then kick you out? Give you the cold shoulder with no explanation? Completely lie to you the entire time I've known you? I have too many options to choose from so I settle on the simple. "I'm sorry."

"Can I ask you a question?"

"Of course."

"What are you so afraid of?"

I decide to answer this one honestly. "Everything."

He doesn't respond for a few long seconds. Then he glances over at me, his face dark except for the glow from the dash. "You know you can trust me, right?"

Trust. Such a flimsy thing. So hard to gain, so easy to lose.

When I think about it, I realize I can't answer that question. Do I really trust anyone?

I can't answer.

Too quickly, he's pulling up in front of my house.

"Thanks for the ride." I unclick the seat belt.

The light is off and darkness shrouds the porch like a giant cloak. I pause for a moment, unable to help myself, and assess the dark house I'm walking into alone. Not that I'm afraid of a burglar or anything, but Gravy has been known to ambush me. When Paige is home, she usually distracts him from his sneak attacks on my legs.

Jared notices my hesitation. "I'll walk you up."

"That's not necessary."

"It would make me feel better with everything that's been going on lately."

He leaves the engine idling and his headlights on as we walk to the front door.

He takes the lead up the sidewalk and I'm not going to complain because he looks very good from the back.

But because he's in front of me, and because I'm too busy ogling his butt, he sees it first.

He stops walking, forcing me to a halt behind him. "What is it?"

"Did you . . ." He gestures to the door.

It's standing wide open.

"No." I shake my head.

"Is Paige home?"

"No. She stayed the night at Naomi's."

He nods and walks back to the car.

I maintain my position on the sidewalk, my gaze fixed on the open doorway. I can't see anything inside, it's too dark.

Is someone in there?

In the background, Jared is on his phone, giving someone Ruby's address, then turning off his car. Then he gets his gun. He doesn't hold it up or cock it like they do in the movies; instead he just holds it pointed at the ground.

Then he heads for the open blackness of the front door. "Stay here."

"I'm not staying out here in the dark by myself." I follow him up the porch steps.

"I promise you won't get eaten by any wild animals."

I almost smile at the reminder of our night in the woods. "You're still not leaving me out here alone. What if it's a serial killer and he's just waiting for you to go inside so he can sneak out and murder me?"

"I don't think it's a serial killer. There have been other incidents like this and no one was hurt."

"So then I'm safe to go in with you."

He sighs. "Fine. Just stay behind me."

We enter the shop slowly and quietly, Jared leading the way.

"Are you sure you didn't accidentally leave the door open when you left?"

"No way, I'm entirely too paranoid and—"

There's a howling shriek as Gravy bolts out the front door, making me yelp and latch onto Jared's arm.

"You okay?"

How can he be so calm? "I'm fine." But I don't release his arm.

Jared flicks on the lights.

The shop is still and empty.

"Everything look normal?" he asks.

There's no sign of damage, and nothing appears to be missing. The register is closed and locked. The ledger that I left out on the front desk is unmoved. "It looks the same as when I left."

"That's been the MO."

We move further into the house, with Jared turning on lights as we go.

Nothing in the hallway. No sounds other than our soft footsteps, our light breathing and the click of the light switch.

But then we get to the kitchen.

Jared turns on the overhead lighting and I freeze.

Lying on the counter is a single red rose.

5

———————

Fifteen minutes later, a tired and rumpled Jared is sitting in my kitchen. Our hands are wrapped around mugs of tea.

After we discovered the rose, Jared inspected the entire house top to bottom. Once he determined there weren't any murderers lying around, he had me check for anything that might be missing or out of place.

Anderson arrived while we were upstairs, minutes after Jared had called him. Anderson is still here, trolling around for any signs of damage or anything else the intruder might have been up to. Besides leaving behind the single rose.

It has to be the parents. Who else could it be? Are they involved in all of the other incidents around town? Why would they be breaking into houses without taking anything? And why leave evidence they were here in the first place? None of it makes any sense.

If they are in town, Paige and I need to leave. I can't

risk them finding her. Taking her from me. But we can't leave right now, not with Jared sitting here staring at me.

"Do you know of anyone who might have left the rose for you?" Jared asks.

"No." I take a sip of my tea. "What did they find at the other crime scenes?"

He hesitates before answering my misdirection, watching my face for something.

Does he not believe me?

"A few had nothing left behind, just objects moved around the household or left in odd places. At Mr. Godfrey's, they found one of those little plastic swords they use for drinks. At Eleanor's, there were a bunch of leaves and honeysuckle flowers scattered on her counter and floor."

Someone else had something floral? I relax a little bit. Maybe it's a coincidence. A super creepy coincidence, but a coincidence nonetheless. Although I don't believe that. The call and now the rose? It's too purposeful.

He stands up and opens my freezer.

"I don't think the perp is in there."

He pops back out to give me a dry look and then sticks his head back behind the door. "I'm looking for anything out of place."

"Like what?"

"Spoons."

"Spoons?"

Apparently there's nothing in my freezer of interest because he shuts the door with a frown.

"Or other objects. All the other crime scenes had weird things in the freezer or sweaters with the sleeves tied in knots. Did you notice anything like that?"

"No. Why would someone break into a house to put spoons in the freezer?"

He sits back in the chair across from me. "Your guess is as good as mine." He lifts both brows at me. "Do you have any guesses?"

"Not a one."

"Unfortunate. If this is anything like the other cases, Anderson won't find anything."

I shiver and hug my arms around myself.

"Either way, you can't stay here alone."

"I'm not alone. I have Gravy."

"Gravy welcomes intruders. And pretty much anyone but you. He'd probably aid and abet the perpetrator if there was an attack on you."

"Ha ha, that's funny but no one is going to attack me."

"What if this person comes back? What if these seemingly harmless incidents escalate?" He leans forward, his eyes piercing mine. "What if someone is scoping out places to rob later and Paige is home alone?"

I frown. "I won't let her be alone. And that's a lot of what-ifs. I can't shut down the shop. I'll have to be here during the day at least."

"I know, but still. It might not be safe." He drums his fingers on the table, a line between his eyebrows as he frowns down at the floor for a second before meeting my eyes. "You should at least go somewhere else for tonight. You can stay with me."

"What? No way." We'll never be able to sneak out of town if we're staying with Jared. Plus, living in the same space, seeing him at night before bed and in the morning when I wake up, accidentally running into him after a shower when he's in nothing more than a towel . . .

"Why not?" he asks.

I shake my head to clear thoughts that are quickly descending into madness. Sexy madness. I absolutely cannot stay with Jared.

"I can stay with Tabby tonight. I'll let Paige know in the morning."

He's silent for a moment, watching me, his eyes seeking something in my face, maybe if he can convince me further. He doesn't like what he sees. His eyes shutter and he looks away. "Fine. I'll call her."

The drive to Tabby's is silent and awkward. I clutch my overnight bag in my lap in the front seat of the patrol car.

Jared's knuckles are nearly white, wrapped around the steering wheel.

He parks in front of her house and gets out to walk me to the door. Tabby's racing down the walkway before we've even exited the vehicle.

"Are you okay?" She's wrapped in a thin pink robe.

Her hair is tied on top of her head in a dark, messy bun and she throws her arms around me.

"I'm fine." I shift my overnight bag over my shoulder. "I'm sorry to wake you in the middle of the night like this."

She shushes me with a hand. "Don't worry about it. I was already up. What happened?"

"When Jared dropped me off, the front door was standing wide open, even though I locked it when I left. That's about it."

"What a trip." She turns toward Jared. "You better catch this guy before the whole town starts freaking out."

He runs a hand through his already-rumpled hair. "Too late," he mutters.

"Come on, let's get inside and you can tell me all about it." She grabs my arm and drags me toward her house. "Bye, Jared," she calls over her shoulder.

Jared stands next to his car, watching us with an inscrutable expression. I give him a small wave, and before the door slams shut behind me, he smiles. But it's a sad smile. My own lips falter.

Fortunately or unfortunately for me, no time to think about that.

"Ben and I had sex," Tabby blurts.

We haven't even made it past her entryway. Apparently, her concern isn't about me. "And?"

"And? That's all you have to say? *And?*"

"I'm confused. Haven't you guys already had sex, like multiple times?"

"What? No!"

"Really?" I scrunch my face at her. "That seems highly unlikely."

"We've . . . messed around before. We were make-out buddies only." Now she's wringing her hands and pacing.

"Can I put this stuff down somewhere—?"

"But then, things got a little more intense and it just happened. And then it was weird. Now what am I supposed to do?"

I have no idea what to tell her. She's upset, insecure probably, and she wants me to help her. I'm not sure I know how to console people who aren't thirteen-year-old girls, and even with Paige I suck. But then again, I sat with Mr. Bingel when he was sad about his wife and son. I helped the boys when they were distraught. I could be like a life coach or something.

Or not.

I swallow. "Go open a bottle of wine. I'll meet you in the living room."

A few minutes later we're sitting on her couch, wine in hand.

"Start from the beginning," I tell her. "What exactly happened?"

She cocks her head at me. "Well, we were fooling around and then he put his tongue in my—"

"No, no!" I hold up one hand in the air to stop the words coming out of her mouth. "I don't want to know about all that. I mean, what happened afterward to make you all freaked out? You said it was weird?"

"He wasn't weird per se." She grimaces. "He left."

"He left? Without saying anything?"

"He said it was nice."

"Nice? What does that mean?"

"I don't know." Her hands flail. "This is why I need help. What do I do?"

"When did all this happen?"

She bites her lip. "About an hour ago."

"Tonight? He was here tonight? And you guys had sex for the first time? Tonight?"

"Would you stop saying that? Yes. We had sex tonight. He came over after he closed up the bar and . . . you know. And it didn't take very long. And then he left."

She puts her wine glass down and starts pacing again and mumbling to herself. "I knew this was a bad idea. I should have listened to him from the beginning. But I had to get all handsy and we had to go and do this and now everything is going to be awkward. Troy is going to be pissed. He might kick Ben's ass or my ass or both our asses and then we can never be friends again ever." She flops down next to me with a groan. "What have I done?"

"I think you're exaggerating, just a little. It's not going to be that bad."

"Not that bad? We had sex! Then he said it was 'nice.' " She grimaces, then covers her face with her hands. "It's terrible!"

"Maybe nothing will change," I try.

"That would be even worse. But you're probably right. He's going to act like nothing's different. I hate him."

"Or maybe he likes you too much, and he panicked and that's why he left." I can relate to that scenario.

Her head tilts as she considers my words. "Maybe he does have feelings for me. Maybe I have feelings too. Maybe I love him."

"I don't think you should make any rash decisions. At least, not tonight. If you sleep on it, things will seem better in the morning."

She deflates a little against the couch. "You're probably right."

I lean over and put my hand on her shoulder. "Tabby, I've seen you guys together. Trust me when I say Ben likes you more than he lets on. I can tell."

"You really think so?"

"I do."

"Thank you." She pats my hand on her shoulder.

I sit back and take a sip of the wine.

She sighs. "Sorry to take over the night. Now it's your turn. Tell me about you and Jared. What is up with all the tension there?"

"Tension? There's no tension."

She rolls her eyes. "Please. There was so much tension between you two I could walk it like a plank." She brings the wine glass up to her lips.

I decide to throw her a bone. "He wanted me and Paige to stay with him."

The wine glass sinks back toward her lap. "He did?"

"Yeah, but I told him to call you instead."

She frowns. "Why didn't you stay with him?"

"Are you crazy?"

"Pssshhh. You're calling me crazy? You're an idiot."

"I'm the idiot? I'm not the one who slept with Ben."

She tilts her head and purses her lips. "Touché. Well. At least we can be idiots together. But you cannot sit there and pretend like Jared asking you to stay with him means nothing."

"You know how Jared is. I'm sure he would have offered the same to anyone who lived alone."

"*Au contraire, mon frère.* Eleanor had someone bust into her house, and he didn't invite her to sleep with him."

My face heats. "He didn't ask me to sleep with him."

She toasts me with her glass. "Whatever. Here's to men who don't want to sleep with us. Or who think it's *nice* to sleep with us. Ugh, has there ever been a more terrible word in the history of the English language?"

"Um, yes. Orifice."

She grimaces. "Okay, that one's pretty bad."

"Fecal."

"Ugh." Her mouth twists.

"Moist."

"Okay, moist is where I draw the line." But now she's laughing. She throws her arms around me. "Thanks for making me feel better. I am so glad you're here, Ruby. What would I do without you?"

I'm glad she can't see my face as I pat her back.

6

———

Two days later, Paige and I are still living at Tabby's.

We tried to leave. "Tried" being the operative word. I've been stashing money under a loose board in Ruby's bedroom. It's not much, but it might have been enough. We made it exactly a block and a half when the car stalled out and died. We had to push it to the side of the road and leave it. Which means we're still in town.

Even though there haven't been any more clues from the parents, I can't shake the need to run. What if they show up and claim Paige, accuse me of kidnapping? It wouldn't be a baseless charge. Legally, I have no right to custody.

On the other hand, if they're already here and keeping tabs on us, will they just follow us wherever we go anyway? How did they find us to begin with? If I take Paige somewhere new—which I can't yet afford, especially without a car—will they follow and take her? Are we safe anywhere?

Despite the anxiety, staying at Tabby's is actually kind of fun, except there are only two beds so either my legs get kicked all night (Paige) or my ears get assaulted all night (Tabby).

It could be worse. Even though I'm exhausted, we cook dinner together, watch movies at night after work and laugh a lot. Tabby gives me some of her clothes, insisting they were things she was planning on getting rid of anyway, but I think she's lying to me.

She felt bad after seeing most of my pitiful wardrobe, which consists of a few shorts and T-shirts, one pair of pants, one set of PJs, and a couple of dresses Ruby left behind.

I don't argue with her too much, she's a little shorter than me, but most of the tops and summer dresses she gives me fit just fine.

She's been totally great about everything, except I feel like we're intruding. Especially since Ben hasn't come around to talk and I think Tabby is worried he's not making an appearance because she's too busy with her houseguests—us. She plays it off like it doesn't bother her, but I see the tension in her eyes and her mood has been more subdued than normal.

In the meantime, I've made mild inquiries to Mrs. Olsen about new people in town, but she doesn't know of any new residents around my parents' age. Although being nearly summer, tourist season is picking up, so they could be blending in.

After I told Paige about the rose, we decided to set up the cameras around Ruby's property. That way, we might be able to catch anyone lurking about the place.

Two days later, there hasn't been any activity on the cameras except for Mr. Bingel and the boys and the mailman.

But if the parents are in town, they're watching us somehow.

"Maybe it's a coincidence," Paige tries after we've reviewed the tapes at Ruby's and found nothing unusual going on. "Roses are common flowers. And you said someone else had flowers, too."

"Not a rose, though. At the other house, it was more like they'd rolled around in a bush and tracked in leaves and stuff. This was placed specifically on the counter where I would see it as soon as I walked in the kitchen."

"But these things are happening all over town. Not just to us. It might not have anything to do with them."

In addition to the cameras, I've been checking the phone periodically—it gets one bar of service at irregular intervals when I leave it in the register drawer—and there haven't been any more calls.

Maybe Paige is right and everything will be fine.

Doesn't stop the impending sense of doom lingering in my consciousness every day.

I need to get involved in the investigation in case the police uncover anything that leads to the parents, or clues as to whether they are in town or not. Something to decisively link them to the break-in at Ruby's, maybe even the other incidents throughout town. But I already told Troy I wouldn't help, and since refusing to stay with him, Jared hasn't talked to me. How can I get them to ask me for help...again?

Book club is Wednesday night at Tabby's house. Paige can't handle all the old ladies and immediately disappears to the guest room to do homework. There are at least a dozen women—mostly over the age of seventy—sitting in Tabby's living room, drinking tea and discussing the novel. Which means talking about it for a minute and then going completely off topic.

They're all dressed up for the event, in either skirts or dresses, with full make-up and hair all curled and styled. The cloying smell of various perfumes permeates the air, mixing with the vague aromas of hairspray and mint. It should be terrible to be stuck in a small room with heaps of old ladies, but instead, it's almost comforting. Homey. It's like something you might remember about your grandparents after they're gone . . . people who know their grandparents. I've never known any family other than Paige and the parents. I can't imagine them as children. Sometimes I think they were sprung fully formed from the depths of an inferno.

"Did you think it was weird that one of the aliens was named Horny?" Mrs. Olsen asks.

"It wasn't weird," Tabby answers. "It was intentional. The character has a horn, and it's a horny book, you know?"

"Did you say it was corny?" Miss Viola yells.

At least three people turn toward her and shout, "Turn up your hearing aids!"

Miss Viola doesn't say anything. I have a feeling she hears them just fine but chooses to ignore them.

"I can't believe we're having this conversation," I say.

"Did you hear about Mr. Hutchison asking Gladys St. Claire out for coffee?" one of the ladies asks.

There's a murmuring hum around the room.

"It's about damn time," Mrs. Olsen says. "Some people are averse to romance around here." She gives me a pointed glare.

I sip my tea and try to change the subject. "So about these aliens . . ."

"I heard from my neighbor that there have been a bunch of burglaries around town. Have you heard anything about that?" Mrs. Hale asks Tabby. Mrs. Hale's hat today is teal and covered in bright, fake daisies.

"Why would I know about that?" Tabby asks.

"I saw your brother over at Mr. Godfrey's apartment. When I asked why he called the cops, he told me he wasn't the first one to report an 'unusual occurrence.' " She makes air quotes with her fingers. "But he wouldn't tell me what it was. He never shares anything." Her mouth twists like she's tasting something sour.

"Oh maybe that's the same thing that happened at Eleanor's," Mrs. Olsen says.

"What happened there?" someone asks.

"Well, I don't know exactly, but Eleanor told me someone broke into the house, but nothing was taken or missing."

"Then how does she know someone broke in?"

"Stuff was moved around. And there was a toilet brush in the freezer."

So that's what Jared was looking for in my freezer.

"In the freezer?" someone asks.

Mrs. Hale gasps. "Maybe it's aliens."

"Why would aliens put stuff in the freezer?" I ask.

"Why *wouldn't* aliens put things in the freezer?" Tabby chimes in, acting like this is the most normal topic ever. She tosses me a bright smile with a wink.

She is entirely too amused by this whole conversation.

I'm glad they don't know that someone also broke into my place. I would never live it down.

Mrs. Hale flutters a hand to her chest in what could be fear or excitement, I can't tell. "Maybe they're doing advanced reconnaissance before an invasion. They came to our planet to impregnate our females!"

Gasps and excited murmurs fill the room.

"What do you think, Ruby?" Mrs. Olsen asks me. "Have you had any visions?"

I shake my head. "Um. No."

"She had a break-in the other night," Tabby volunteers on my behalf. "And didn't Troy come over and ask you to help them?"

Tabby's sitting next to me, making it easy to elbow her in the ribs.

"No, I didn't and no, he didn't."

"Ohhh," Mrs. Olsen points at me. "You have to help them."

"No, I don't."

"Yes, you do, then you can report everything going on back to us."

The rest of the room whips their heads in my direction. Then everyone is talking at once.

"Maybe we could all help with the investigation."

"I love a good mystery."

"Our next read for the book club should be a mystery. Do they make any mystery books with lots of sex?"

I stifle a groan and settle for giving Tabby a death glare. "Look what you started," I whisper.

"Sorry," she grumbles, nudging me with her shoulder. "This is fun though, right?"

"I bet the intruder is a ghost," Mrs. Hale says. "Last week, I saw an apparition over by the ruins on the cliffs. It's the old ghost of Captain Donahue, looking for his lover, Francesca Dubois."

Murmurs skitter around the room.

"You were drunk," Mrs. Olsen says.

"I was not," Mrs. Hale retorts, her tone offended. "I saw it clear as day, some kind of being, all white and glowing in the moonlight."

"What are they talking about now?" I ask Tabby out the side of my mouth.

"Some old urban legend. Captain Donahue built the castle that Castle Cove is named after. Only a collection of rocks and stone are left up there now."

I nod. "I've seen it from the boardwalk, but I've never been there. How do you even get to it?"

"You can get there either from the beach and a hike

up, or from the park and a hike down. It's kind of a pain either way."

"We used to have fun there when we were kids." Mrs. Olsen nods at some of the other ladies.

The women titter and talk and I have to raise my voice to be heard over the chatter. "What's the legend about?"

Mrs. Olsen turns toward me. "You've never heard the story?"

"No."

That sets everyone into another tizzy.

"You can't live here and not know the story about the castle," someone says.

And then everyone is talking all at once, shouting about pirates and sheriffs and some other nonsense that I can't quite make out over all the voices.

"Everyone quiet!" Mrs. Olsen makes a shushing noise. The chattering fades. "I'm going to tell the tale.

"Two hundred years ago, Castle Cove was a major port for the shipment of goods on the West Coast. There were a ton of sailors who came in and out of the cove, but of all of them, Captain Donahue was the most famous. He was a world-renowned merchant, known for his frequent brushes with death and blind luck with pirates. He had the castle built as a place to stay when he docked here, since this was his main port. He was also a handsome man. He could have anyone he wanted, but when he saw Francesca Dubois, his heart was irrevocably tied to hers forever."

"Tell her how they met," Mrs. Hale commands.

"I'm getting there." Mrs. Olsen wrinkles her noise in Mrs. Hale's direction. "Francesca was a barmaid. She worked at the local tavern for old Iggy Azalea."

I toss Tabby a look. Did she mean . . .

Tabby stifles her laughter with a hand and elbows me in the side.

Mrs. Olsen keeps talking, impervious to our amusement. "Francesca had moved to Castle Cove alone, and no one knew where she was from or what brought her here. She was very beautiful. Dark hair, olive skin, like some kind of gypsy. She sent all the local men into tizzies. They vied for her hand, but she evaded all of their advances. Until one night, Captain Donahue visited the local tavern. This wasn't normal for him. He always stayed at the castle, he wasn't the type to dally around with barmaids, but something brought him out that night. He was immediately taken by her beauty. She was smitten by him as well, but she didn't show it. She couldn't show it. She wanted the captain, but she had to do her best to stay away from him. You see, Francesca had a secret."

The women in the room are riveted.

"What was her secret?" I ask when Mrs. Olsen's dramatic pause lasts a little bit too long.

"She was wanted . . . for murder!"

A few gasps fill the space.

Tabby snorts. "Like they haven't already heard this," she mutters.

"Who did she kill?" I ask.

"Her husband. He was abusive and he totally

deserved it. But there was a sheriff from Baker County who had been searching for Francesca, and she had to keep to herself and not draw attention. So even though she fought against her attraction and pushed Captain Donahue away, he wasn't swayed. He pursued her relentlessly. Every time he was in town, he would eat at the tavern and ask Francesca to come away with him. She always said no. But one day, finally, after fighting their desire for months, she gave in." Mrs. Olsen shrugs. "He was an honorable gentleman. And he was super hot. Hard to resist. Plus, the sheriff was getting closer, and she knew she would have to leave town anyway. She wanted to live life with the captain while she still had a life to live."

I shift in my seat. All of this sounds uncomfortably familiar. Minus the whole murder thing.

"I'm guessing they didn't live happily ever after." All eyes flick toward me. "Because of the whole . . . haunting thing," I finish lamely.

"You are correct, Ruby," Mrs. Olsen says. "The day the captain and Francesca had planned to run away together, the sheriff from Winston County arrived. He followed her to the castle and confronted her on the bluffs. The captain saw them from his window, but before he could make it down the stairs and out the front door, Francesca flung herself off the cliffs." At the word *flung*, she flings her own hands through the air, very nearly knocking Mrs. Hale's hat off her head.

Miss Viola jerks awake at Mrs. Hale's protest.

Undeterred, Mrs. Olsen continues, "The captain ran

out of the castle and attacked the sheriff. They fought at the edge of the cliff hour after grueling hour, equally matched in skill and strength. One would start to get the edge on the other, but the other would always come back even stronger. Until finally, the captain slipped on a rock and pulled the sheriff with him to their deaths. They say when the moon is high, you can still hear the sounds of Francesca Dubois and Captain Donahue calling in the darkness, trying to find each other."

There's a beat of silence.

That's it?

"Everyone died?" I ask.

I'm more emotionally invested in this story than I should be, considering it happened two hundred years ago, and Mrs. Olsen is absolutely exaggerating, if not outright lying.

Still. I'm thinking I should stay away from cliffs. And captains.

"Everyone died." Mrs. Olsen nods and then looks around the silent room. "Let's bring out the cake."

7

———

"**I**'m not going to make it home for dinner tonight," Tabby tells me when she answers Troy's phone. It's nearly six, so I called Troy's house to find her.

There weren't any leftovers from book club the day before, so our choices for dinner are grilled cheese or cheese sandwiches. They're totally different things. They just happen to have the same ingredients. Hence my call to Tabby for her preference.

"Troy is sick," she adds.

"Um. Troy is a grown man," I say. "Look if you want to bang Ben again, just say so. Paige and I can make ourselves scarce."

"That's not it, for reals. Troy is sick and I have to take care of him."

"Seriously?" He doesn't seem the type to moan over a little snot.

"You don't understand. He practically cuts off his foot

and insists it's just a flesh wound, but the minute he has a cough it's like he's dying. Plus Mom always made him this soup . . ." She doesn't say what I know she's thinking —since their parents retired and moved away, Tabby's the only one that can make the soup. "I can't leave him when he's like this. He's pathetic."

"I can hear you," Troy says in the background.

He doesn't sound sick. She's probably fed up with us and making excuses so we don't feel bad. I hate having to infringe on her like this.

An idea strikes. With a bit of maneuvering and manipulation, I can solve two problems at once.

I hang up with Tabby and then pull a rumpled piece of notepaper out of my purse. The paper Jared gave me with his number on it. I take a deep breath and dial.

"Reeves," he answers almost immediately.

"Hi, Jared. It's Ruby."

"Are you okay?"

"Yes, everything's fine. I just wanted to let you know that Paige and I are going back home, so if you're patrolling and you see the lights on over there, it's just us. No need to call in the troops." I laugh like it's a joke.

"What do you mean you're going back home?"

"Well, Tabby is staying with Troy because he's sick and it's been a few days since the break-in and there haven't been any more issues. I doubt the intruder will return to the scene of the crime."

"Wait, hang on." There's shuffling and muttered cursing and then he comes back on. "You're calling me from Tabby's."

"Yeah, we're going to pack up right now and—"

"No. Stay right there. Don't move."

He hangs up.

When I put the phone back on the receiver, I'm smiling.

Less than an hour later, the doorbell rings.

I answer the door.

"Hey." It's Jared. Of course.

He's wearing black shorts, a T-shirt, and a baseball cap on backward, making him look about five years younger. His skin is a light gold from the late-spring sun. Why does he have to be so hot? If he would just look a little less amazing, it would make it so much easier to use him without the lingering pang of guilt in my chest.

"Hi," I say before immediately adding, "We're okay by ourselves."

My protests are token. If we stay with Jared, I can get in on the investigation, or I can at least get more information on these break-ins and determine if the parents are connected.

He smiles. "You guys are staying with me for now. There's no way I'm leaving you alone with everything that's been happening."

It's almost too easy. "What's been happening? No one has gotten hurt."

"Yet."

"So, no one has gotten hurt yet, and no one probably will."

"Probably?" He lifts his brows.

On cue, Paige emerges from the back hallway. "Hey. What's going on?"

"You guys are staying with me for a few days," Jared says.

"No, we're not," I say.

"I have a pool," he counters.

"I'm going to get my stuff," Paige says before scampering back down the hall.

I let out a defeated sigh. "Fine." I turn away from the door. "I have to go pack."

I already packed, so once I get to the back bedroom, I linger a few minutes to keep up the ruse.

When I'm done pretending, I find Jared and Paige waiting for me on the porch. I lock up the front door with the key Tabby left me and we get in his car.

"We're going to stop and get Gravy," Paige tells me. When I grimace, she adds, "Jared said it was okay."

Of course he did.

We stop for the devil cat and his food, and then we head toward Jared's house. He lives east of town, more inland.

"Staying with me won't be so bad," he says.

"I know."

Is he kidding? It's a necessary evil, but it's going to be torture to have to see him all the time. To know how close he is. To hear him in the shower, naked. Not that you can hear nakedness but I'm sure I'll picture it.

Hell, I'm picturing it now. I force myself to look out the passenger window.

He clears his throat, and when I glance over at him, he's looking at Paige, his eyes meeting hers in the rearview mirror. "I called the school. The bus driver is going to stop at the end of my street to pick you up tomorrow."

"I can't walk?"

"I live too far away, just outside city limits."

"Okay," Paige says. "Thank you."

We're silent for a few minutes except for Gravy purring loudly on Paige's lap in the back seat.

I sneak a few peeks over at Jared while he drives, his profile steady in the glow of the setting sun. Crossing my arms over my chest, I force my gaze back out the passenger window.

The further we get from Castle Cove, the more the scenery changes from beachy sand to towering pines.

After a few minutes, he pulls off the main street and down a gravel road. Our surroundings become even darker.

"You live all the way out here?" Paige asks.

"It's not too far," Jared says.

The gravel road opens up and circles into a driveway. Next to us is a sprawling house.

"This is your house?" I'm frozen in the passenger seat.

"Home sweet home." He gives me a sidelong grin.

It's bigger than I expected. This isn't some quaint cabin in the woods. This is practically a mansion.

The house is wood sided, a sprawling single story with soaring windows and a giant wraparound porch.

We get out of the car and Jared grabs both our bags from the back seat, slinging Paige's over his shoulder.

"I have two guest rooms, so you can each have your own bed." He's walking in front of me up the steps so I can't see his face. He fumbles with the keys before opening the front door and clicking on a light.

"Wow." Paige enters behind me.

We're in an open entryway with vaulted ceilings and gleaming wood paneling.

He puts our bags on the floor.

"The kitchen is through here." He walks over to a doorway and turns on another light, illuminating the kitchen. It has granite counters, dark wood cabinets, and recessed lighting that glints off the stainless-steel appliances.

"Feel free to take whatever you want from the fridge. It's stocked up with drinks and snacks and whatever you might need." He rubs the back of his neck. He won't look straight at me.

"Jared."

He focuses on me.

"This place is amazing. You live here all alone?" I hadn't meant that as an accusation, but once the words are out, it sounds like one.

He shrugs. "Eventually I'll have a family to fill it up." The words are quiet but firm.

Now I'm the one who can't meet his eyes, thinking about the person who will help him fill this house with children. It won't be me. I can't even imagine it. The criminal and the cop. What a joke. Not that he was insinuating I would be the one to help him with . . . whatever.

"Where's the pool?" Paige's voice breaks into my thoughts. Her eyes are bright, her voice high and excited. "Can I go swimming now?"

"Um . . ." I look over at Jared for an answer.

"Have you guys eaten dinner?"

We exchange a glance.

"No," I answer.

He nods. "I'll show you the pool. You can swim and I'll barbeque some steaks or something. Sound good?"

"Sounds awesome." Paige's whole face is glowing.

She's never going to want to leave.

"I'll show you to your rooms," Jared says.

We pick up our bags and follow him out of the kitchen and down a long hallway.

He shows us the spare bathroom, which is bigger than any "spare" thing I've ever seen. The room has high windows, double sinks, a giant walk-in shower, and a separate garden tub.

Paige's room is painted a light blue with pale wood furniture. There's a wide window overlooking the lawn with an extended view of trees and sky.

I think she's been struck speechless because she nods at us with a dopey smile on her face and then shuts the door to change.

My room is one door down on the opposite side. It looks like something out of one of those fancy mountain-retreat hotels, more wood and a large four-poster bed covered in a colorful quilt. It also has a French door that opens onto the back patio where the pool is, although I can only make out the far corner of the pool from where I'm standing.

This doesn't seem possible. How does a cop have such a great house? The pay scale in Castle Cove can't be that good. Everything here is expensive and high quality, without being oppressive or pretentious. High-end, but nothing like what our parents would choose.

"Thanks, Jared." I throw my bag on the bed.

"I'll go get dinner started," he says from the doorway. And with a smile and a nod, he disappears back down the hall.

I shut the door and slump on the bed. I haven't been sitting there contemplating this turn of events long before there's a gentle tap at the door.

Paige pushes into the room and flops onto the bed next to me. She has her swimsuit on. "You have a view of the pool? Lucky."

"This place is . . ."

"Amazing? Fantastic? I never want to leave, ever? Yeah, all those things," she says. "He must be loaded."

"Paige!"

"You know you're thinking it, too."

I am. But I don't want to.

8

———

I don't have a bathing suit—not that I plan on getting in the water anyway, but I can stick my feet in with the best of them.

By the time I change into a tank top and shorts, I can already hear Paige splashing around in the pool. She's always loved the water and I've always feared the water. Well, not always. Mom pushing me in really didn't make me warm and fuzzy about it though.

I peek out the French door. From this vantage, I can occasionally make out Paige's head as she swims back and forth. She's talking to Jared. I can't see him, but I can hear the rumble of his words in tandem with her lighter, brighter voice.

I have a few minutes alone in his house. I step back from the window. I shouldn't do it, but I'm too curious to stop myself. I'm not going to completely snoop around; I just want to get a little more of an idea about the man behind the badge.

I dart out of my room and head down the hall, away from the kitchen and toward the other rooms. Behind one door is an office. It's a fairly simple space, a thick wood desk, a top-of-the-line computer, and a wall full of books. There's a degree on the wall with Jared's name on it from the University of Chicago and a couple of plaques commemorating his service.

The next door down is the master bedroom. The space is large and bright, the furniture sturdy and similar to the other rooms' stuff. It's not how nice it is that surprises me. What surprises me is the lack of anything personal. Don't get me wrong, the house is awesome, but it's missing personality. I had hoped my snooping would give me a little insight into Jared, but this room is as blandly nice as the guest rooms. There are no family pictures on the walls, no laundry haphazardly thrown on the floor, or clutter on the dresser. Every surface is bare and dusted. There's no indication that it's even lived in. In fact, the whole place feels more like a comfy hotel than a home.

I glance inside the master bath. There's a wide walk-in shower with multiple nozzles and a Jacuzzi tub surrounded by windows that overlook the forest—nothing but green trees and grass.

When I turn back to the bedroom, I notice the one small picture in the room, on the bedside table. I pick up the photo and trail a finger around the metal frame.

It must be his parents. They're standing next to each other, the man's arm around the woman. His gaze is on her, while her eyes are focused on whoever holds the camera. They're both laughing, their eyes bright and happy. Jared has his dad's smile and his mother's eyes.

Swallowing, I put the picture down and head back out toward the kitchen.

The windows in the kitchen are open—overlooking the pool and back patio.

Paige is still splashing around in the pool while Jared stands at the grill, flipping steaks. The whole backyard is as beautiful and impressive as the house without being too extravagant. Slate surrounds the lagoon-style pool, and the grill is attached to a long granite counter with a mini fridge.

The patio has a variety of wide chaise lounges with fluffy cushions. A fire pit doubling as a table rests between some of the seats. Beyond the pool is a large expanse of grass tapering off into the tree line. There probably isn't another house for miles.

Even though the sun has set, there's still a slight glow in the sky and it's fairly warm out.

"Will you grab the veggie kebobs from the fridge?" Jared calls out to me when he spots me loitering in the kitchen.

"Sure." I turn to the large fridge and open one side, which is the freezer instead of the fridge. A stack of frozen meals, the microwavable kind, rests on the top shelf.

I open the other side and it's stuffed with food. The kebobs are on a tray right in the center, skewered with a variety of veggies: bell peppers, pineapples, onions, mushrooms, and various squashes. On the bottom shelf,

I spy a range of drinks—everything from juice boxes and sodas to water and wine. Did he buy all that stuff for us? I can't imagine him buying juice boxes for himself. He must have picked them up for Paige.

I grab the tray of kebobs and shut the fridge but pause again and open the freezer, my eyes on the frozen meals. There are enough prepackaged meals in there to last a few weeks. Is that how he normally eats? Did he go through the trouble of filling his fridge for us?

I shut the freezer and take the tray of veggies out to the porch.

"Is the water cold?" I call out to Paige. I hand the tray off to Jared.

He's changed into swim trunks and a tank top, showing off his muscular shoulders.

Not that I'm looking.

"The pool is heated," Paige calls back, lifting her eyebrows, clearly impressed.

"Do you need help?" I ask Jared. He's already putting the veggies on the grill with a set of long metal tongs.

"Nope. We're all set here. Why don't you have a seat and relax? Do you want a drink?"

"I'm okay." I'm glad he doesn't need help. I can barely cook with an oven, let alone man a grill.

I sit in one of the fluffy chaise lounges and watch Paige. After a minute, Jared sits next to me.

"So what's going on with the case? Do you guys have any new information?" I ask. I'm so fishing.

"I'm sorry." He doesn't sound sorry at all. "I'm afraid I can't make comments on an ongoing investigation."

"Really?" I wrinkle my nose at him.

He shrugs. "You can change that. I know Troy asked you once to help us. I'm sure you would get the same terms as last time."

I blow out a breath, like I'm really thinking about it first. "Fine. I'll help you guys. Tell me what you know. Don't leave anything out."

He's silent for a moment, his eyes twinkling in the lights from the pool. "There's really nothing more than you already know. I was messing with you."

I stare at him and then laugh. "I can't believe you lied."

"I didn't lie."

"You totally did."

"I did not. All I said was that I can't make comments in an ongoing investigation. That's the truth."

"Maybe not an outright lie. But you misled me."

His mouth tilts to the side. "Maybe. I was planning on doing follow-up interviews with the victims, if you want to tag along."

"Are you going to interview me, since I'm a victim?"

He shrugs. "I thought you would do the whole," he waves his hands around, "whatever you did the last time."

That surprises me. "The whole thing where I accused Mrs. Hale of stealing cupcakes when you were really buying them for her?"

"Well, maybe it didn't work out so well that one time. But I have to admit, you did see something you shouldn't have known about. This time might be better. I have faith in you." He's smiling, teasing me. But the words bother me.

He shouldn't have faith in me.

Dinner is excellent. The steaks are cooked just right, and Jared even found time to prepare a salad. We eat on the patio, Paige wrapped in a towel, wet hair dripping onto the chair cushion, but Jared doesn't seem to mind even though the patio furniture is almost too nice to even be outside.

Jared and Paige chat about school. There's a teacher who has to be a hundred years old, because she taught when Jared went to the same school and she looked just as old then. They also talk about the weird noises that always echo from the vents in the bathrooms and the ancient books in the library.

"What do you want to do when you grow up?" he asks her.

She shrugs and I don't miss the glance she sends my way. "I think I want to be a veterinarian."

"Oh, really?"

"Yeah. I love animals."

It's true, I've always known she loved animals. Even when she was younger and I would take her to the park or whatever, she would go crazy over people's dogs and animals. Hence Gravy. But I had no idea she wanted to be a vet.

I wonder if she's telling the truth about her dream occupation. I had no idea she had aspirations to work with animals. I don't know why she didn't tell me before.

Maybe because we can't afford to send her to college. Hell, I should be in college right now.

I guess there are always student loans. Maybe if we find a place to live where we can actually stay for a long period of time, she'll get good enough grades to get a scholarship. The dream is nice.

Our conversation ceases while we're all chewing our food, and then Paige glances around and asks, "How can you afford all this anyway?"

I choke on a piece of salad. "Paige!"

"It's okay," Jared tells me. "My parents died a few years ago. I was an only child, so I inherited the house."

"Your parents must've been rich," Paige says.

I try to give her a death look, but she won't meet my eyes.

"They did all right." He wipes his mouth with his napkin, which draws my gaze to his lips.

He's such a strange contradiction. He lives in this awesome house but drives a ten-year-old Jeep. The mercenary side of me, the part that's always sizing people up, wonders if he inherited any money in addition to the house, but I'm not about to ask and I'm a terrible person for even thinking about it.

Once we've finished eating, we all help carry the dishes into the kitchen.

I insist on washing them.

"I don't cook much more than premade frozen meals or grilled cheese," I tell him. "You have to let me do something. You can keep Paige entertained."

His eyes light up. He turns to Paige. "Wanna play Marco Polo?"

"What's Marco Polo?"

"Were you raised under a rock? Come on, I'll show you."

From the kitchen window, I watch them laughing and playing. He's so great with Paige. It makes my heart hurt. And when he strips off his top, exposing his lean, muscled torso, and dives in the pool, other parts of my body start aching right along with the beating organ in my chest.

I'm not sure how long I'll be able to live with him without jumping his bones. The sooner this mystery is solved, the better.

9

The enticing smell of bacon and coffee rouses me from a slumber fit for the dead. I can't believe I didn't wake up once. No snores from Tabby jolting me from my sleep, no heels in the kidneys from Paige, no Gravy jumping on my face and trying to smother me in my sleep. Out here it's as silent as a morgue except a lot more cozy.

When I roll over and look at the clock, it's after seven.

Oh, crap. Paige has school today. The bus is supposed to be here in fifteen minutes.

I fly out of bed and down the hall, knocking on her door. "Paige, we're running late," I call out.

I'm startled by her voice coming from down the hall instead of inside the room.

"Jared woke me up. He's taking me down to meet the bus in a couple minutes." She's dressed and ready, her backpack slung over one shoulder, a piece of bacon in her fingers.

"Oh," I say. "Right."

She disappears from view. I can hear their voices murmuring and Paige laughing.

This is too weird. I'm not used to having someone . . . I don't know, help with my responsibilities.

After taking care of nature and retying my wild hair, I follow my nose and the delicious smells to the kitchen.

Jared grabs his keys off the hook, dressed in his running shorts and tank top. "I'm going to take Paige to the bus stop. I made bacon and pancakes." He gestures toward the counter. Those damn tank tops. His damn arms. He cooked me food and he's taking care of Paige like . . . like . . . I don't know, like he cares.

I nod, not yet ready for coherent speech.

"Did you sleep okay?" His head tilts, maybe sensing that I'm about to dissolve into a puddle of goo at his feet.

"Mmmshermmfer."

"What?" His eyes return to mine, and this time they're concerned.

"You're fine. I mean, I'm fine. I mean, I slept fine."

Dear god, kill me now. If I could smack myself in the forehead without looking more insane than I already do, I would.

"Good." He smiles. "I'll be right back."

When the front door bangs shut, I sag against the counter. I need to get a grip.

I'm halfway through stuffing my face with pancakes when Jared returns.

"I figured we could shower and then you can do the whole reading thing." He pours himself a cup of coffee at the counter. "Do you have to be at the store, or can we do that here?"

I'm still stuck on his first sentence. He probably doesn't mean together, but that's what gets lodged in my brain.

"We can do it here. Did you need to take your run?"

"I went earlier so I could wake up Paige for school." He's facing me, leaning back against the counter with his coffee.

"Ah."

I finish up my pancakes while he heads to his room to get ready for the day.

It would be nice if I had some kind of information to give him, but I've got a whole lot of nothing. We took the cameras down after the Castle Cove Bandit, or Bandits I should say, were caught and placed with Mr. Bingel. We didn't want to risk the cameras being found after their usefulness had ceased. I suppose I'll have to act like my chakras are blocked or something and no visions can come through. Or I'll just wing it.

When I make it back to the kitchen after getting ready and throwing my hair in a messy bun, Jared is talking on his phone. He's changed into dark jeans and a gray T-shirt.

He's usually so put together, his hair trimmed, his face shaved. His clothes are always flawless, simple but high-quality material hugging his body like it was made for him.

Then there's me. I haven't dyed my hair in six

months. My roots are growing out, the ends are getting frayed, and my clothes are used and slightly too small.

Okay, so Tabby's tank top and shorts are nice enough, but next to him I feel like a homeless street urchin.

"Right," he says to whoever is on the phone. "See you then."

He hangs up and turns to me. "That was the chief. He has a copy of the case files ready and waiting down at the station so you can go through them. I thought we could talk to some of the victims first thing this morning, see if you can get a read on anything, and then I'll drop you at your place if you need to open the store? On the way home tonight, we can stop at the station to get the case files."

I nod in agreement. "That sounds good. Thanks."

He says "home" so casually.

"Oh and I gave Paige the code for the garage so when the bus drops her off this afternoon, she'll be able to get inside."

"You've thought of everything."

He shrugs, brushing me off.

"Where should we . . ." I look for a place to sit and open our chakras—or whatever I told him last time. All I remember is that I was totally trying to mess with him.

"How about the living room?"

When I nod, he leads me into the next room. The room has large overstuffed couches and a giant flat-screen on the wall. I sit on the larger couch and he sits next to me, angling himself in my direction.

Just like last time, he puts his hands out in front of him and I put mine over his.

It's the same thing we did before, but this time it's absolutely not the same.

I can't concentrate on being Ruby. All I can think about is the warmth of his hands against my fingers and the faint pulse in his wrists.

He's a runner and in excellent shape. I expect his heart rate to be low—under sixty beats per minute, maybe, but the pulse flickering under my fingers is decidedly faster.

His eyes are closed.

I didn't even have to tell him this time.

I watch him for a few long seconds, his heart beating through my fingers. I run my gaze over the angle of his jaw, the sharp curve of his cheek.

Am I making him nervous? Excited?

Staring in silence probably isn't the wisest course of action. He opens his eyes and catches me watching him.

His pulse goes a little faster.

A brow rises. "Are you getting anything?"

"No. Maybe it's the space." As good an excuse as any.

"Oh." He frowns slightly.

"Let's keep trying. Shut your eyes."

He complies and I continue staring at him, mind blanking. "I see . . ." I swallow. "Keys."

"Keys?" His eyes are still closed, and there's a crease between his brows.

Okay, a total shot in the dark on my part, but someone must have a way to get into these houses without having to break in. There's never a sign of forced entry, only the door left hanging open. And picks would leave scratches cops would recognize in a heartbeat. I'm making things up at this point. It's like Occam's Razor: the simplest explanation is likely the correct one and someone is probably using a key to get in.

"Lots of keys. Does that mean anything to you?"

"No."

"Hmmm . . . I also see white hair."

Not really rocket science. More than half the town has white hair.

A brow lifts even though his eyes remain closed. "That doesn't really narrow down our targets."

"Someone has the keys," I intone.

"Who? Someone with white hair?"

I pause, pretending to think about it. "I don't know. Maybe."

We're silent again for a few long moments and then I sigh and give up.

"I'm not getting anything else."

He squeezes my fingers lightly and then pulls back. "It was worth a shot. Well, let's go talk to some people. Maybe something will come to you."

"Absolutely." I slap a confident smile on my face.

Ugh.

Mr. Godfrey is our first stop. The same man who came to the shop, looking to get rid of the ghosts and the little people. He lives in senior housing, which basically looks like a normal apartment complex except they have a communal dining room and a nursing staff and they go on weekly excursions.

"I've already told you, it was the little people. They sneak into houses at night for their sugar and babies." Mr. Godfrey booms so loudly I bet the neighbors can hear everything he's saying. He didn't invite us in. We're standing in his doorway while he recounts his information.

"Were you missing any sugar?" Jared asks.

He considers my question. "I don't think so."

"What about babies?" I can't help but add.

Jared coughs and turns away for a second.

"I don't have any babies," Mr. Godfrey bellows. "But ever since I bought your sorcery and witchcraft items, I haven't had any issues." He nods at me, his expression both satisfied and suspicious.

"Did you notice anything moved or missing?" I ask.

The moustache twitches. "My dishes were washed."

"Someone broke into your house . . . and cleaned your dishes?" I glance over at Jared, but he's making notes in his little book.

"That's right."

Why they couldn't do some of my household chores when they broke in? This trespasser is weird.

"Did you have any flowers or roses left around?" Jared asks.

"Roses?" Mr. Godfrey thunders. "Why would there be roses?"

"Why would there be babies?" I keep my voice low.

Jared clears his throat, trying to hide his chuckle. "I had to ask because there've been other break-ins since yours, and we're trying to find any correlations between the crimes. Will you go over again what happened the night of your incident?"

"Well, I was at the party at the senior center until nine. Then I came home and was in bed by ten. I was sleeping and then . . ." He pauses and rubs one side of the impressively long white moustache. "Then the whole building shook."

Jared and I exchange a glance. The building shook?

"It woke me up. When I came out of my bedroom, the door was wide open, banging against the doorframe. My dishes were done." Mr. Godfrey's loud voice is laced with distress. "I called the authorities. Then you guys came," he nods toward Jared, "and looked around for prints and things, but everything was clean. Even the counters."

We take the faded-white sidewalk back to the car, walking between pristinely mowed lawns and passing the occasional burst of spring flowers. "Anytime anyone wants to break in and clean my house, I would be okay with it."

"It is a bit creepy though."

"Maybe it's a Good Samaritan, trying to help people out," I suggest.

"But they didn't clean everyone's house. In fact, at Eleanor's they made quite a mess. It doesn't really add up."

"Maybe there are multiple trespassers."

He shrugs. "Possible, but seems unlikely. Multiple intruders, same basic MO? And such a weird one at that."

Our next stop is Eleanor's. She lives in a small duplex near the center of town. It's a quaint building, yellow with white trim and a neat garden.

She invites us in, coughing, and then apologizes. "I'm getting over a cold." She has a napkin clenched in her hand and her nose is slightly pink.

"Tell us what happened," Jared says once we're in her living room.

Eleanor only has one small sofa in her living room so Jared stands while I sit on the couch next to Eleanor. Her house looks like her. Everything is dainty and organized. Her bookshelf is arranged by book height and color. One of her shelves has knickknacks, all in a row and shiny. There's not so much as a dust bunny in sight.

Our place isn't nearly as neat. Ruby's shop is clean, but cluttered, and Paige and I tend to live on the messy side. There's always a dirty cup or three scattered around, Paige's shoes in the middle of the living room, and extra blankets on the couch for when we're watching movies.

I glance over at Jared for his reaction to her place. Is he comfortable here? Has he been here before? I can't really tell, and I can't stare too long because he asks her to tell us about the break-in.

Her hands are in her lap, one clenching the other.

She's wearing a short-sleeved blouse buttoned up to the neck.

"I woke up last Friday morning and everything was a mess," she says.

"Did you see any roses, or was there a rose lying around anywhere?" I ask.

Her cheeks turn a bit pink. "No. There were some dried leaves and honeysuckle flowers on the floor by the front door, and on the counter."

Why did she blush at the mention of roses?

"Anything else?" Jared asks.

"The couch cushions were on the floor, there were spoons all over the counter in the kitchen, and my wall clock was in the sink." She gestures to the wall where a round clock with a black cat hangs, the eyes and curled tail clicking back and forth, marking the seconds as they pass.

My eyes are drawn to a small crystal dish on the counter below it. It's full of what appear to be individual-sized ketchup packets. Just like the one Troy had in his pocket.

I direct my attention back to Eleanor, my suspicions rising. The other night at trivia, it was Troy's idea to take Eleanor home. In fact, now that I think about it, he was planning on driving her home and then offered to drop me off first, even though she lives a bit farther out than I do and he would have had to backtrack to take her home last and then go to his house.

She's getting over a cold, and he just got a cold. Hmmm.

"You saw the damage the next morning?" I ask. "None of the noises woke you up?"

Her cheeks get redder. "I'm a heavy sleeper."

"You must be a really heavy sleeper if someone came in and moved all this stuff around and you didn't hear anything."

She nods and gives me a weak smile, not meeting my eyes. "I already talked to Officer Reynolds about all of this, you can ask him."

Right. I bet he knows *all* about it.

I glance over at Jared to see his take on this. It couldn't be more obvious. But his expression is blank.

I can't help but glance back over at the ketchup on the counter and the tissue in her hand. Did the mention of roses make her blush because of Troy?

"Right. Thank you for your time."

Once we're outside, I turn to Jared. "She's lying."

"Why would she be lying?"

I watch him carefully. I'm pretty sure there's never been anything serious between Jared and Eleanor, even though Mrs. Olsen has been trying to hook them up for years, according to Tabby. But he did show up at the bar with her the other night, and even though I still don't think it meant anything, I don't want to be the bearer of bad news if he is emotionally invested, even a little bit. The thought of him having any kind of emotion for Eleanor makes my stomach twist in ways I don't want to examine too closely.

"I think we will get more answers from Troy," I say vaguely. "Let's go see the patient."

Jared's heated stare warms my face as he starts the car, but I avoid making direct eye contact.

Troy's house isn't too far from Eleanor's, and it's larger than her little duplex. It's a two-story house with dormer windows and green shutters.

When we knock on the door, Tabby lets us in. Her hair is pulled back in a messy ponytail, her clothes are stained, and her eyes are wild. "Thank god you're here. He's driving me insane." She steps back to let us into the house and then calls down the hallway, "Jared and Ruby are here. I'm taking a break." And then she leaves, slamming the door behind her.

"She didn't even have shoes on," Jared says.

"I don't think she cares."

The sound of coughing followed by a groan filters down the hallway.

I expected Troy's house to be more of a bachelor pad with sports paraphernalia, old beer cans, and manly dark wood walls.

Instead, it's homey. The ceiling is vaulted, and the walls are cream colored and decorated with a few carefully placed pictures of his parents and Tabby. We pass by an open doorway to a quaint kitchen with dishes stacked in the sink, and there's a curving staircase that must lead up to bedrooms.

I follow Jared down the hallway into the living room, where Troy is laid out on the couch under a thick blanket littered with crumpled tissues. His nose is red and his eyes are puffy.

Hm. I thought Tabby was exaggerating his illness to get away from us. Maybe I was wrong.

"You look like shit," Jared says.

"Thanks a lot." Troy's voice is raspy. "Where's Tabby?"

"She saw blue sky and bailed," I tell him.

Troy nods and then coughs again.

Jared and I exchange a glance.

With a half shrug, he sits in a chair next to the couch.

"We wanted to ask you about Eleanor." Jared glances up at me for confirmation.

I nod.

Troy coughs again, but this time the sound is forced. "What about her?"

Jared looks over at me, brows raised.

I sit on the arm of the couch next to Troy. "Where was she really the night of the break-in at her house?" I keep my gaze fixed on Troy, not sure if I want to see Jared's expression when he pieces together what I figured out at Eleanor's.

Troy sniffs. "How should I know?"

Jared is quiet, staring at Troy, his face as blank as ever. I look from one to the other, wondering if Troy wants to keep it secret because he's afraid to upset his friend.

"*Troy.*" I use my mean-mom voice, which has some effect on Paige. "I know you're hiding something."

"This is the result of all your psychic prowess? It led you to *me*, the most honorable, decent, and honest man in this town? I think your Ouija board is off."

"Even sick, you got jokes." I pat his foot. "But it's time to come clean."

His eyes flick over at Jared and then he winces.

Jared's eyes widen. "You and Eleanor?"

"It's not like that," Troy says quickly. "We're just . . . you know, having fun," he mutters.

"Was she at your house the night of the break-in at her place?" Jared asks.

Troy nods, the movement quick and brief.

"That's why she was lying," I say. "Wait, that doesn't really explain why she was lying." Unless she's trying to protect Jared, too?

Troy frowns. "She's private. She doesn't want anyone to know we were together."

"And you were going to tell me about this when?" Jared asks.

"I wasn't sure how you would react."

"You would lie during an ongoing investigation to protect her privacy?"

"It wasn't that." He stops and runs a hand through his already-rumpled hair. "I didn't— I wasn't sure if you had feelings for her."

There's a heated pause and then Jared laughs. He just throws his head back and roars, exposing his strong throat and white teeth. "You thought I wanted her?"

"Well, Mrs. Olsen has been trying to hook you guys up forever. I wasn't sure how you felt about the matter, but I thought for sure Eleanor was into you. The whole thing came as a surprise to me."

Jared laughs again, quieter this time, and shakes his

head. "I've never wanted her. If I did, I would have done something about it."

I can't help but stare at him. The words make my heart clench in my chest. If he wanted me, he would have done something by now, too. Well, we did make out that one time. And I was the one to push him away, but still. He's probably over me. Too bad I wish he were under me.

Ugh, my brain. What is wrong with me?

Troy's quiet for a moment. "She doesn't want everyone to know." He looks at Jared, then over at me.

"I won't say anything," I promise.

Jared shakes his head. "I wouldn't share that information either, you know that."

"I know, but if she put it in her report, more than just you and I would have access to the information. You know how Anderson is. The man loves gossip almost as much as he loves cheese. So I promised not to say anything. To anyone. I'm sorry, man. I should have told you, even if it was left out of the report."

"Fine." Jared nods.

The radio on his belt chirps and a voice cackles over the line. "Is anyone near Dr. Allen's office on South Birch Street? The Newsomes are in there again."

My brows lift. The doctor's office?

Jared sighs and stands, heading outside to respond to the call.

When I look back at Troy, he's pursing his lips at me. "Did your psychic senses tell you about me and Eleanor?"

"Absolutely," I say quickly. "By the way, what's with the ketchup packets?" I may be blowing my secrets, but I really am curious.

He smiles slowly. "It tastes better from the little packets than it does from the regular bottle. Eleanor always goes over to Roseburg to purchase new books for the library. They have a McDonald's and she always stops there to bring me back the ketchup."

"You are so weird."

"You know, you're pretty observant." He tilts his head and watches me, his eyes assessing despite the redness from his illness.

Time to change the subject. "When are you going to let Tabby leave so we can move back in with her?"

"You really want to leave Chateau de Jared? That place is like Disneyland for adults. Speaking of, how's that going? Have you guys boned yet?"

I give him my most unimpressed look. "Seriously?"

"Sorry. If I didn't ask while I had you alone, Tabby would kill me."

"I don't know why she's so hell-bent on hooking us up."

"You really have no idea?" Troy asks me before grabbing a tissue from the box next to the couch and blowing his nose, the trumpeting delaying my response.

"What do you mean?"

"You know what I mean. The guy has it bad."

"Has what bad?" My voice escalates into a squeak.

His brows lift and he rolls his eyes at me. "You're staying in his house. No one ever stays there."

Heat creeps up my neck. "Only because Tabby"—me —"forced the issue."

He glances over at the doorway. "He's not the same." He keeps his voice low.

"What do you mean?"

"I mean . . . I've known Jared for nearly my whole life. For the last few years, Jared's been different. More serious. He sort of lost himself after his parents died, you know? And I really never thought he would snap out of it. But lately he's been so much more— And that's why I think the duckbill platypus is the greatest of all the platypi."

I turn. It's Jared.

"Tabby is out there practically talking in tongues. You think you could give the poor girl a break?"

"Fine. Leave me here, all alone, sick, uncared for," he presses the back of his hand to his head, "unloved."

"I think you'll survive." Jared turns toward me. "Are you ready to go?"

"Yeah." I stand. "I hope you feel better soon."

Outside, Tabby is sitting on the lawn with her legs crossed.

"What are you doing?" I ask.

"Trying to find the Zen because I hear sibling-cide is frowned upon in these parts."

"Right. Carry on." Jared guides me toward his car, his hand on the small of my back.

"You think she'll be okay?" I ask when we're driving down the road.

"He's always overly dramatic when he's sick and it rubs off on Tabby, since she has to deal with it."

"You've seen this before?"

"He gets sick at least once a year. So yes. Every time." He smiles at me.

We're quiet while he directs his car toward Ruby's.

I can't help the curiosity zinging through me about what Troy said. The thought Jared might have any kind of feelings for me is simultaneously thrilling and terrifying. I mean, obviously, since the whole make-out thing, I can tell he's physically attracted to me. At least somewhat. Enough to stick his tongue down my throat. But could it be something more than that? How *could* it be more than that? He doesn't even know me. Not the real me. Would he feel the same if he knew the truth?

After Jared drops me off, I open the shop and deal with a few customers. There are also some more shipments to unpack. I've been replacing our more popular items as we run out, keeping track of the profits and the best-selling items for when Ruby returns.

A couple of tourists stop in and I give one a reading.

Then I sort through the mail, which is mostly a stack of invoices. But there's one odd piece of mail. A postcard.

I pick it up, wondering if it's for me or the real Ruby. Maybe it's from Ruby, although I'm not sure they have postcards at ashrams.

On one side is a picture of Roseburg, the largest town

only an hour or so away. On the other side, there are only five words.

The first word is my name. Not Ruby's name, but my real name, written in sharp script. *Charlotte.*

Underneath, a very clear, seemingly innocuous message.

We'll see you soon.

And then underneath that, a smiley face.

It's not signed, but it doesn't matter. I would know the handwriting anywhere.

Mother.

My eyes travel over the card, taking in details. The postcard isn't stamped.

They were here. Or they sent someone here with this message for me.

Denial is futile.

I scramble up the stairs to the computer to review the video, even though I have a sinking feeling I know what I'll find: a whole bunch of nothing. Heart pounding, I replay the tapes from the night before, fast forwarding through the boring bits and stopping only when there is movement. I go through the tapes twice. Nothing. Just flashes of Mr. Bingel and the boys in their yard, a couple of customers I recognize, and then the mailman dropping off letters. They must have somehow gotten the postman to deliver it without a stamp.

I could find out.

It's about lunchtime anyway, so I lock up the store, flip over the sign that reads *Out to Lunch*, and walk toward downtown.

The post office is across from the boardwalk, right on the main drag. It's one of a dozen storefronts. The entire expanse of shops features a barber sharp, a restaurant, a jeweler, a used bookstore, and more. The post office itself is small, a single counter over which one employee hunches, filling out paperwork, and a narrow room extending back with a wall of mailboxes.

"Hi." I smile and wave at the person at the register, and I recognize him as the same man who delivers my mail every day. His name tag reads *Roger*.

"I was wondering if you could help me . . ." I trail off, not really sure how to ask what I need. I really should have thought this through more.

"Yes?" he asks after a few long seconds.

"If someone wanted you to deliver something without a stamp, how would that work?"

He frowns. "If you want to mail something, you need a stamp."

"I know, but . . . well, I got a postcard in the mail today, and it wasn't stamped."

"Maybe someone put it in your mail slot."

"I don't—"

I cut myself off. Now he's looking at me like I'm crazy. I don't want to tell him I used video surveillance to rule out that possibility.

I glance behind the counter to where the mailbags are.

"Could you show me how the whole mailing process works?" I try.

His eyes brighten. "Well, sure. It's pretty simple actually. We have a truck that brings in shipments every day. I sort it here and then divvy it up into the different routes. We have two trucks. I take the north side and my co-worker Carla takes the south side. And that's about it."

"So if someone were to, say, slip an unstamped piece of mail into one of the delivery bags from the truck, would it be noticed?"

He pauses with a frown. "Well now, I've never thought about that. The distribution center is in Roseburg. That's where everything is scanned for postage before it's sent here."

I nod. "Right. Thanks for your time."

I walk back home, mulling it over. They could have easily slipped their postcard into either the post office or the mail truck, or the delivery truck even. The fact that they took the time to send it without the postage stamp is telling.

They want us to know they are close, that they could appear at any time.

10

Jared picks me up at five, once the shop is closed, and we go to the sheriff's office to pick up the case files.

I've never been inside a police station before. My shoulders tense as we walk through the door, even though the building itself is innocuous enough. Nondescript brick lines the outside and hard carpet the inside, which is accented with furniture that looks like it survived the eighties with only a few scrapes and dings to show for it.

I meet the chief for the first time, who is entirely too excited to see me.

"I'm so pleased to have you here." The chief pumps my hand so hard my teeth nearly rattle. "You've been a real asset lately with everything going on."

Chief Sanders is an older gentleman, a bit rotund in the middle, with a perpetual smile on his face and a white beard. I bet he dresses as Santa Claus every year.

I wish I could see it to prove the theory, but I'll be long gone by then.

His desk is cluttered with paperwork. At the corner sits a framed photo of his family, him with his wife and a few grown children.

I smile and make small talk, but it's hard. All I can think about is that damn postcard.

Finally the chitchat ends, and we get the file and head out.

As we're driving to Jared's, my mood must be tangible.

"Is everything okay?" he asks.

"Everything is great." I smile and ask him about his day, anything to get him talking so I don't have to think about what I'm going to tell Paige.

He talks about looking at a map of the incidents to try and find a connection, but I only partly listen. The postcard is burning a hole in my back pocket, like the words are embedding themselves into my skin.

See you soon. With a smiley face!

Like they're welcome. Like they're normal. Like we're some kind of ordinary family that's been separated briefly but actually wants to be around each other.

This is just like them.

Always pretending.

"Hey, is that a mechanic?" I cut Jared off midsentence when I spot the building. From what I can see as we drive past, there are a few bays for oil changes and such and a ton of junked-up cars in the rear.

"Um. Yeah. I saw your car parked down the street. Does it need work?" he asks.

I nod slowly.

What I need is a different car to leave town with to help throw the parents off our track. I wonder if I could get some kind of trade for a vehicle that's actually running. Anything to get us out of town.

"It's no big deal. Sorry I interrupted you. You were saying?"

I pay attention this time, and I agree to go over the information with him after dinner tonight.

When we get to Jared's, Paige is already inside. She's in her room doing her homework.

Jared goes into his room to change out of his uniform.

Perfect. I need to get this over with.

"Paige." I shut the door behind me.

She's lying on her belly on the bed with her books and notebooks spread out around her. She looks like such a normal teenage girl.

And I'm here to ruin it all.

She smiles at me, but the smile drops when she sees my expression. "What's wrong?"

I pull out the postcard and hand it to her.

She reads the words quickly and then flips the card over, looking at the picture with dismay that mirrors my own before she flips it back over to the words.

She scrambles to sit up on her knees and throws the postcard on the bed. "This sucks."

"That about sums it up."

"We have to leave." Her voice is laced with resignation and tears.

"I'm sorry, Paige. I know we hoped the phone call and the rose were flukes but this is sort of irrefutable."

"I know." She crosses her arms over her chest. "What are we going to do?"

I've been thinking about this all day. "We have to prepare to leave, obviously," I say. "As soon as possible. But . . . we need a reliable form of transportation."

It would have been easier to leave from Tabby's house, if we had stayed there. Instead, I forced us over to Jared's not only to get involved in the investigation—because I probably could have managed that from anywhere—but also to try and make Tabby happy. I've gotten way too soft.

I push the thoughts away. There's no changing it now. "I have an idea. They've got to be watching and waiting for us to bail. Why else send us these messages? I'm thinking we'll have to do a middle-of-the-night exit, but we need to prepare and be careful. We can't just bolt. That's what they're waiting for. I'm keeping the cameras up and I moved one of them to cover the street, to see if any suspicious vehicles or people are keeping an eye on the house. We need to figure out where we're going to go. It would be nice to have a destination in mind. For once." I rub my eyes, exhaustion overwhelming me. I wish we had passports or something. Maybe then we could go to Fiji. "I want to come up with a plan, something to mislead them. Something to make them think we're going one way while we actually go another. You know?"

"Um. How are we going to do that?"

I sit down on the bed next to her. "I have no idea. We're probably safe here at Jared's for at least a little while. He has a security system, and he's a cop. I don't think they'll do anything while we're here."

"Then we should stay here forever," she says with a weak smile.

She knows as well as I do that's never going to happen. I shake my head.

"I don't understand how they found us." She wipes her eyes. "Can we at least stay until summer break? That's only two weeks."

I look at her tear-streaked face and nod. "We'll plan for after school ends, it's a Friday. We have to pretend like everything is normal until then."

She nods, her mouth set in a straight line. "I have a school dance that night."

"Maybe we can leave right after the dance. That would be the perfect time. If they know you're going, they'll know I'll have to pick you up. We just need the car. Then we can leave straight from there, pack the car earlier . . ." My mind is running through possible scenarios, trying on ways to show them one hand while the other is putting an ace up my sleeve.

"Oh, hey," she interrupts my train of thought. "I heard something today that might be helpful to the case."

"What is it?"

"Some older kids were hanging out at the bluffs, you know, by the castle? They thought they saw something or someone out there. They said it was a ghost, but you know." She shrugs.

"Hm. Mrs. Hale also mentioned seeing someone out there."

"Maybe whoever is playing these pranks goes out there to play pranks, too."

"Thanks, Paige." I give her a sideways hug. "You've done good."

She smiles, but she's not as thrilled as she normally is about contributing to these types of shenanigans. "Are you scared?"

"Of course I'm scared, I don't want them to find us."

She nods and then watches me, her eyes still bright with unshed tears. "Maybe you would be better off without me."

"What? Why would you say that?"

"If you didn't have to worry about me all the time, you would have gotten away from them ages ago. You'd probably be off somewhere, married or doing something you love instead of constantly running."

I put a hand on her shoulder until she looks up at me. "Don't say that. Don't ever say that. I would not be better off without you. I need you, Paige."

"Why?"

"It sounds so cheeseball, like something Danny would tell DJ and Stephanie while the laugh track is on pause."

She smiles. "Say it anyway."

"I love you, Paige. And I don't love just anyone. You're important to me."

She hugs me, wrapping her skinny limbs around my waist. "I love you, too," she says with a sniff. "You're the best sister. I'm sorry we have to keep running away because of me."

"If I were on my own, I'd still be hiding from our parents. They're the bad guys here, Paige. Not you. Never you."

She nods, seemingly mollified for the moment.

I leave her to her homework.

In the living room, Jared is sitting at the couch with a map spread open in front of him on the coffee table.

"Hey." He stands when I enter the room. "Is Paige all right?"

"She's fine."

"I thought I heard her voice. She sounded upset."

I watch his face carefully. Did he overhear what we were talking about?

"She's okay." I wave my hand dismissively. "Teenage girl stuff. What's all this?" I nod toward the map.

"This is where all of the incidents occurred."

I sit next to Jared and glance over the information. There are five red dots on the map. "They're all pretty close." Except for Ruby's. I mean, it's not too far—nothing in Castle Cove could be considered far away—but it's definitely not on the same path.

I lean forward to trace a finger over the spots. There are Mr. Godfrey and Eleanor's places. There are two more dots; one was a vacation home that is currently empty, but a neighbor reported the front door left open. There was no damage, just a roll of toilet paper unfolded all over the entryway. The fourth dot is more of the same. The owner is currently out of town for a few weeks.

"These are the bluffs. Where the castle is." I point at a rounded section of the map that's marked as a state park. The dots make a somewhat straight line, one less than a mile from the bluffs and the rest moving south, pretty close together.

"Yeah. The castle is situated about here." He points, his finger millimeters from mine.

I turn toward him, thinking about how to present the information I have. "I feel like . . . there's something there. Something happening at the old castle that might be connected to the incidents."

He watches me for a few long seconds and then shakes his head. "You always surprise me."

"What do you mean?"

He rubs his chin. "Mrs. Hale called the station last week and reported seeing someone out there. They sent Troy to check it out, but it was only some teenagers messing around. They also reported seeing something."

I nod. "Yeah."

"So you think the same person who's been trespassing in people's houses every week could be doing what, exactly? Haunting the bluffs and impersonating a ghost in their spare time?"

"Well, maybe not. But do you think it's worth looking into?"

He considers my question for a moment and then nudges me with his shoulder. "If you really want to hang out with me on a starry night next to the ocean, all you have to do is ask."

"Ha ha. But seriously, we should check it out. Did anyone say what nights or what times they saw the night roamer?"

"No." He shrugs. "But Mrs. Hale is usually in bed by ten."

"When should we go?"

"I don't want to leave Paige alone," he says.

My heart does a little flip. The strange organ reacts oddly every time he talks about Paige like she matters.

He continues, "She wanted to stay over at Naomi's on Friday. We could go then?" His eyes meet mine, the question lingering in his gaze.

"Um . . ." I hesitate.

"What? You have other plans?"

I smile and this time the motion isn't so forced. "No."

Despite my exhaustion, I can't sleep. I can't stop thinking about everything.

Our parents. Where are they? What are they going to do? Will they ever leave us alone?

And then there's the leaving itself. Where are we going to go? Last time we ran off, we hid out at a seedy motel until we found a place to live. We might have to do the same thing again. I am not looking forward to scratchy sheets and junk food.

What will happen in Castle Cove when we disappear? Ruby will return, and they'll find out I was lying all along.

What will Tabby think?

What will Jared think?

My stomach twists.

Sick of lying in bed with my tumbling thoughts and increasing anxiety, I slip out the door and onto the patio. The porch lights are off, but the pool lights are on, casting a wavering, bluish glow into the cool night. I pad over to the water and sit on the edge, slipping my bare feet in. The water is bathwater warm and soothing. I take a deep breath and shut my eyes.

"Can't sleep?" a voice says.

I twist around.

Jared is walking out of the kitchen door. His swim trunks hang low on his hips and he has a towel thrown over his shoulder.

"You too?"

He tosses the towel onto one of the lounge chairs and stops next to me. Even his feet are well formed. His toes are clean and straight. My eyes linger on them before moving up to his strong calves. I force my gaze to the water in front of me. You know you have a problem when even someone's feet are attractive.

"Sometimes I can't shut my brain off, you know?" he says.

"Yeah. I get that." So much.

"Swimming helps wear me out."

I nod.

"You want to try it? You haven't gone in since you and Paige got here."

"Oh, I can't swim."

His lips tilt downward and he sits on the side of the pool, sticking his feet in the water next to mine. He kicks slightly, making small waves ripple out.

"You can't swim at all?"

"No. The water freaks me out a little, actually."

"Why?"

"Just, you know, random phobia." I laugh it off, but the sound is brittle.

He doesn't press. His head tilts back as he regards me with those dark eyes. "I can teach you to swim, if you want."

"What? No."

"You know the best way to get over something you're afraid of is to confront it head on." He grins ruefully. "But that's easier said than done."

"Are you afraid of anything?" I ask.

Instead of answering, he slides down into the pool and then turns to face me.

We're on the shallow side. The water comes up to his waist.

He steps in between my legs, one hand on either side of me, so close his thumbs brush my outer thighs.

"I'm afraid of a lot of things," he says, his voice low. "But understanding why you fear something is half the battle." Then he pushes away from the wall.

I watch him swim back and forth across the pool a couple of times. He makes it look so easy, his arms slicing through the water like he's moving through silk. I haven't been in a pool since Mom pushed me in. It angers me that they're the cause of my anxiety. I'm sick of letting them control me. I'm sick of not having a real life because of them. I'm sick of not being able to play around in the pool with Paige because of them. I don't want them to have any power over me, not anymore.

It takes me a minute to gather my courage. I don't own a swimsuit, but I have a sports bra under my tank top and underwear under my shorts and it's basically the same thing, right?

I pull off my top, stand up to shimmy out of my shorts, and then I get in a pool for the first time since I was sixteen. For a few minutes, I stand there in the shallow end, arms crossed and gripping my elbows, just practicing breathing without letting panic grip me.

Once Jared realizes I've entered the water with him, he stops swimming laps, and with two strong strokes he's standing in front of me.

My terror must be showing on my face because he asks, "Are you okay?"

Standing rigidly still, I manage to bob my head once.

"Come on." He holds out a hand.

I stare at it like it might bite me.

He laughs. "Ruby, seriously. I won't let go of you. I promise."

"I'm not so sure about this. I think I'll stand here for a while. You go back to swimming your laps." I wave a hand at him.

"We'll start slow." He moves closer despite me waving

him away. "No swimming or anything, we'll just go in a little deeper."

"I'm not going to the deep end," I warn him. My eyes are still on his hands as he approaches me slowly, like I'm a spooked horse.

"I won't take you there until you're ready," he says. "And I'll be holding on to you the whole time. I promise I won't let go. Do you trust me?"

I meet his eyes, steady and unwavering on mine. Then I nod.

With the uncanny sensation that I'm stepping off a precipice into a void, I reach out and take his hand.

He talks to me. I don't register all of the words, but his voice is low and soothing and he rambles on while guiding me a little deeper, where the water hits just under my ribcage.

He's gentle and encouraging, his hands always on me, making me safe even when I finally agree and he takes me into the deeper water where I can't quite reach.

"Look at me," he says when my breathing increases and I start to panic. "Keep your eyes on me, I won't let you go. See? I can stand here."

I listen to his voice, which he keeps low and steady. I keep my gaze fixed on his.

The longer I watch him, the more the panic subsides and I nearly forget I'm in six feet of water.

After a while, he teaches me how to float on my back —while he holds me up—and doesn't get irritated when it takes me multiple attempts to even be somewhat comfortable with my ears in the water.

I'm so nervous about being in the pool, I don't even realize until quite some time has passed that his hands are all over me—not in any kind of lewd way—just there, holding me up, sure and strong on my back, my stomach, gripping my waist with tender hands.

Finally, he lets me go and I float on my back for ten whole seconds before I get super excited, flail, and end up underwater.

Jared is there right away, lifting me up. "Are you okay?"

I wipe my face with my hands before opening my eyes to his concerned expression. I can't stop grinning. "Did you see that? I floated by myself."

His head tilts back and he laughs. "I saw it."

I shake my head, smiling sheepishly. "I'm like an infant."

"No. You're not. You're very brave. Most people who are afraid of the water wouldn't bother trying at all." His voice is laced with humor and something else. Something a little deeper.

"Will you keep teaching me? When Paige isn't around? I want to surprise her." I smile, thinking about it. She will freak out when she realizes I learned to swim. She always wants me to go in the pool with her, but she knows better than to ask.

"Of course." His hands flex against the skin of my stomach.

The movement makes me suddenly aware of our positions. He's holding me around the waist. He's tall enough to be standing on his flat feet, the water up to his shoulders. My hands are on said shoulders, the same ones I've been admiring every time he wears that damn tank top.

Without thinking too much about it, I pull myself closer to him. My legs slide through the water and wrap around his waist like it's the easiest and most natural thing in the world.

His hands tighten around me, holding my thighs. He's not smiling anymore. His eyes are dark and intent, his jaw taut.

I stare at his lips. We move toward each other at the same moment, our mouths meeting in a soft press of flesh.

His arms are rigid under my hands for a few seconds before he relaxes. Then his fingers slide up my back, one hand cupping the back of my head, angling us closer. His other hand is wrapped around my waist, holding me to him.

Nothing exists except me and Jared and the gentle lap of the water heating between us. His mouth and tongue become more insistent and my body responds like a firecracker, heat rushing to my core, making my movements frantic, my hands clutching him to me like he's the only thing that exists.

I didn't exactly have the time or the inclination for boyfriends growing up. I lost my virginity to a guy I barely knew in the back of a Volkswagen when I was sixteen. It was my way of taking control and forgetting about my life for a few brief, and I mean *brief*, moments. It was terrible, painful, and awkward.

This is so far from that, we might as well be in a different galaxy. The heat between us burns, my body about to incinerate, and then he's moving, carrying me up the steps of the pool, my legs still around his waist, his hands gripping my upper thighs. He lays me down on the wide chaise lounge. He's halfway on top of me, still kissing me, but his mouth is now moving down my neck. The air is cold against my wet skin but every part of us that touches is hot.

When he nibbles on the spot where my neck meets my shoulder, I moan.

"Ruby," his breath whispers against my skin.

The word shatters the intensity between us, dropping like a harsh lie shouted into a bed of whispered truths.

That's not my name.

He notices my sudden tension and peers at my face. "Are you okay?" He pushes a wet strand of hair out of my face and behind my ear.

I nod, but the damage is done.

His eyes search my face in the dim light.

"You know you can trust me, right?"

I nod again.

"No, really. You can trust me. With anything."

"Yes," I say.

I don't mean it. I may have meant it in the pool. I know he wouldn't let me drown. But when it comes to the truth of my identity and my past, when it comes to keeping Paige and not losing her to the system, or worse, to the parents . . . I don't trust anyone.

There are some things worse than drowning.

He knows I'm lying, I can see it in the tight line of his jaw and the confusion in his eyes. But he doesn't get angry. I don't think he ever gets angry. He nods, presses his lips against my forehead once, and then pulls back again.

There's something in his eyes that I can't quite process. Tenderness, affection, compassion, understanding . . .

He feels like home.

The thought is terrifying.

As if he can read the fear in my eyes, he stands and helps me up, wrapping me in his towel and walking me to the door leading to my room.

He kisses me once, a brief touch of his lips to mine. There's a whispered good night and then he's gone.

The last thirty minutes are like a dream.

I rinse off in the spare bathroom, get into dry clothes, and crawl into bed, exhausted.

What am I doing? What was I thinking, kissing Jared like that? It's not fair to lead him on when I'm only here for two more weeks.

He doesn't even know my real name.

11

———

The next morning I expect there to be strain between me and Jared, some awkwardness to add to the icing on the crappy cake of my life, but there isn't.

After I wake up Paige, I find him in the kitchen. He smiles at me, a real smile that lights up his eyes and makes my insides flutter like curtains in the breeze.

He makes breakfast while I put together lunch for Paige, just like every other morning. We chat like nothing happened. Like it's any other day and I didn't practically hump him in the pool less than twelve hours ago.

I don't think about his hands gripping my ass when he carried me out of the pool while we talk about how he can give me a ride to the shop on his way to work. I don't think about his hot breath on my neck when we go over our plans to check out the castle at the cove tonight after we take Paige to Naomi's. And I definitely don't think about the slick texture of his skin beneath my hands, the hardness of his chest when it pressed against mine while we're dropping Paige off at the bus stop.

My non-thoughts are making me a bit heated.

To cool myself down, I decide to tell him funny stories about Paige as we're driving into town.

"She was obsessed with super heroes," I tell him. "She made me call her Iron Man. Seriously, I would say, 'Paige put your shoes on,' and she would say, 'I'm not Paige. I'm Iron Man.' " I pitch my voice higher, like a little girl's.

He laughs and then grabs one of my hands, pressing his lips to the back of my fingers before releasing me. The movement is so brief and natural, I can almost deny the entire thing even happened.

I'm still sitting there, speechless, when we pull up in front of the shop.

"I'll pick you up at four." He smiles at me like he didn't pull the rug out from under me with one quick and tender action.

I stare at him while my brain malfunctions. "Okay," I say finally, climbing out of the patrol car.

"Call me if you need anything."

I nod and watch him pull away.

He's dangerous. I need to get a grip on myself. No time for distractions of the sexy variety.

After he leaves, I run upstairs to watch the videos before I open the shop.

There's nothing abnormal, no strangers or anything odd on the tapes over the last twenty-four hours.

I curse and flop my head into my hands. What are they planning? I know they're going to do something, I just need to figure out what. What would I do if I were in their shoes? I try to think of something nefarious, but it's useless. I've never been as manipulative and conniving as they are.

There has to be a way to find them though, or at least confirm they're somewhere in town.

But how?

I tap my fingers on the desk, thinking.

Maybe we should move one of the cameras back out somewhere public. If the parents are nearby, they'll have to show their faces around town eventually. The general store is probably the best bet. Everyone goes there for something eventually.

If I put a camera up there, we might at least be able to determine if they're here, figure out if they have any sort of routine established.

Once that's settled, I call the mechanic's shop we passed the other day and haggle a deal for a car that runs. It's not pretty, a station wagon with a dent in the side and it might not run for long, but at least it runs now. I only have to pay fifty bucks for the exchange, and they will pick up our abandoned vehicle and tow it back to their shop free of charge.

Then I spend some time on the internet, searching for another place to go. Somewhere far away. I wonder if our new car would make it to Alaska.

I putter around on the internet aimlessly, one search leading to another until eventually I find myself researching the origins of the rutabaga instead of looking for places to live.

My heart isn't in it.

My heart is . . . it doesn't matter.

I give up on the search and head downstairs to open the shop.

A couple hours later, I've finished a reading with Mrs. Hale, in which I 've told her absolutely nothing about the future. She comes by once a week to talk about her late husband and her daughter, who lives a few hours away. She doesn't even ask me questions anymore. I think she wants someone to talk to more than anything else. Someone who will listen.

After she leaves, Tabby shows up.

"How's Troy?" I ask her. "Is he still among the living?"

I'm standing behind the register with the ledger open in front of me, documenting Mrs. Hale's purchase of a salt lamp.

Tabby leans against the counter on the opposite side. "He's lucky to be alive. If that cold didn't take him, I was planning on doing the job myself. But yeah, he's better. So I'm going home tonight if you guys want to come back." She says the words casually, but her brows lift and she watches me.

"Oh, that would be a good idea." I nibble at my bottom lip. "But tonight Jared and I are going out to investigate a lead for the case. So maybe tomorrow?" I lean down to put the account ledger under the counter.

"Going out, huh?" She snorts. "You know, you could

keep staying with him. He has more rooms. And a pool. And smoking-hot abs."

My face flushes, prickling with heat.

She points at me. "I knew it!"

"Knew what?"

"You guys are totally into each other, so what's the real deal here, Ruby? Why wouldn't you go for it? Jared is hot, he's single, he has a job, he's hot, he has a house, and he's nice. Plus, he's hot. And he likes you. Time to fess up and pay the pied piper. And by pied piper, I mean sex."

"I'll fess up as soon as you do," I deflect. "Have you seen Mr. It Was Nice?"

She sighs and slumps against the counter. "Ben and I are done. I had time to think about everything when I was secluded from the rest of the world in quarantine. I don't know what I've been thinking, messing around with him all this time. There could be someone who actually, legitimately wants to date me and be with me, and I've been so focused on Ben, who doesn't want anything from me except my awesome boobs. What if I've missed a better opportunity in the meantime?"

"Wow," I say. "Did you tell him this?"

"Well, no. But I'm totally going to."

"Okay."

"No, really Ruby. I mean it. I know no one believes me because Ben and I have been playing this stupid game for years, but this time, I'm really done."

"I wasn't saying okay like I thought you were bullshitting. I really believe you."

She perks up. "You do?"

"Absolutely. You deserve to be with someone who wants to be with you. And I know you know that."

"Yeah." She smiles a little. "I do. And you do too." Her expression turns stern and she points an accusatory finger in my direction. "And that someone is Jared."

I laugh her off with a wave. "We'll see."

Tabby stays for a minute, and we talk and laugh, but she's not quite as exuberant as she normally is. Stupid Ben. I wish there were a way I could help her.

After dinner, Jared and I drop Paige off at Naomi's. Then we head to Castle Cove Park.

Once he parks the Jeep in the empty lot, Jared hands me a flashlight. "We'll need these to hike down to the castle," he explains. "But we should probably shut off the lights once we find a place to hide. That way if anyone is out here, they won't see us before we see them."

"What if they're already here?"

He shrugs. "Not much to do about it. The path is pretty clear, but it gets steep in spots and it's better to be safe and seen than fall off a cliff."

I can't argue with that logic.

The park is small and a bit creepy in the dark. We pass a swing set, a metal merry-go-round with peeling paint, and a small jungle gym. We walk through a larger grassy area and to a small trail leading down the hill. It's so steep, the path switches back and forth in a tight pattern down the slope.

Jared wasn't exaggerating. It does get pretty sketchy in spots and he has to help me so I don't plunge down the hillside.

It's a relief when we finally reach flat ground. From what I can see in the meager glow of our flashlights, the entire clearing is littered with bits of rocks—pieces of the castle. To one side, near the cliff face, are the largest parts of what's left: two large pillars of stone, old turrets perhaps. They're about a hundred yards apart. I follow Jared and we huddle behind one of the large pillars, trying to stay out of the crisp, salt-flavored wind.

Jared roots around in the backpack he brought, searching for something, and I take a moment to scan the area with my flashlight. No one is around. The only sounds are the distant crashing waves and the hum of the wind. Above us there's a wide board spanning between the two turrets. Behind us, on the other side of the column of rocks shielding us, is the edge of the cliff.

On the ground about twenty feet away, I catch a flash of something small and white, next to a rock. I don't stop sweeping my flashlight over it and away. If it's a clue I can use to continue the psychic charade, I'm going to have to take advantage of it.

"What's wrong?" Jared asks. Crap, I must have jerked the light after all.

"I, uh, have to pee." I move the flashlight around again, like I'm trying to find a place to go, but I avoid the area where I saw the flash of white.

"The only bathrooms are back up at the parking lot. Can you hold it?"

I grimace. "No. Will you turn around? I'll go over . . . there." I nod in the direction I intend to go.

"Okay," he says after a beat, and then he turns around.

I pick my way through the rubble of the castle, glancing behind me to make sure Jared is facing away. When I find the flash of white I saw earlier—it's a square napkin with writing on it—I creep around some more rocks until I'm an acceptable distance away. Then I pretend to pee.

This is so ridiculous.

I use the time to examine the napkin. It's from Ben's. I recognize the stamped imprint from his bar, the frog with the crown.

I shove the square into my pocket.

When I'm done fake-peeing I make my way back to Jared. It's cold out here. Even though it's nearly summer, the breeze coming in from the ocean is downright brisk.

"Are you cold?" Jared asks. It's better where we're standing. The rocks help block some of the sea breeze.

"I'm all right."

I should have grabbed a sweater, but it was so much warmer at Jared's house and I wasn't thinking of future comfort, I was thinking about being on a moonlit bluff alone with Jared and playing psychic detective.

He yanks his lightweight sweater off over his head, and in the light of the moon I get a brief glimpse of his abs as his T-shirt pulls up.

Dammit.

He hands me the sweater and I pull it over my head, inhaling the scent of his cologne.

Double dammit.

I might not need the sweater after all. I'm rather flushed, actually.

"Aren't you going to be cold?" I feel mildly guilty for using his sweater. Only mildly because although I have residual guilt for taking his warmth, the little peep show was absolutely worth it.

He waves me off. "I'm fine."

For a few minutes, we stand in the shelter of the crumbling rocks, waiting for . . . I don't even know what.

I can't help but think about leaving. About never seeing Jared ever again. What will he think of me when I'm gone and the truth gets out?

"Jared?" *Maybe I should tell him the truth now.* The thought whispers through my mind like a caress. It would be so nice to unburden myself.

"Yeah?"

"Thank you for everything you've done these past couple of days. For me and for Paige." Who am I kidding? I can't tell him the truth. I can't risk losing her.

"You're welcome. Paige is a great kid."

"She is. She thinks you're pretty great, too, by the way." But maybe I can give him another truth. "She's everything to me. She's all I have left."

We're silent for a minute except for the distant sound of waves crashing against the rocks.

"You never told me how you lost your parents," he says.

"Car accident."

"Huh. Mine too." Car accidents kill over a million people a year. It's really the best choice when making up fake death stories. But for Jared, it's real. I squelch down the niggling guilt.

"You don't talk much about your parents, either."

"Not much to talk about. They were awesome parents. The best. Then they were gone. Drunk driver fell asleep and crossed into oncoming traffic."

I wince. Sorry is so inadequate. Especially when my own story is a lie. "That sucks."

"Yeah."

"You're an only child?"

"Yep. Sometimes I wish I had a sibling. Someone to share the memories." He pauses. "And the pain."

"It's hard to bear that on your own."

He nods.

Thankfully, he doesn't ask for any further clarification on the demise of my parents. I don't know if I could stomach telling more lies in the face of his very real pain.

A fleeting thought gives me pause: if he actually looked anything up about the real Ruby, he would find that her parents are alive and well and she doesn't have a little sister.

Hopefully, if he hasn't searched yet, we should be in the clear.

"Would you think it was . . ." He scrubs a hand through his hair and looks away. "Never mind."

"Would I think it was what? You can't start a sentence like that and leave it." I nudge him with my elbow.

"Paige is important to you, right? You would do anything for her?"

"Absolutely," I say without hesitation.

"She's really bright, too. And you guys have a lot going on with the store and making ends meet. Wouldn't it be great if she had some money set aside for college?"

I have no idea where he's going with this. "Well, yeah. That would be great." He's mirroring my thoughts from the other night when Paige mentioned veterinary school.

He's silent for a few long seconds. In the gentle glow of moonlight, his face is dark, his bright eyes searching for mine. "Would you let me put some money aside for her in a college fund?"

I nearly fall over. "What?"

"I want to give you some money for Paige. For college," he repeats.

"But I—"

"I know you don't like it when I help you," he interrupts. "But hear me out. You'd really be doing me a favor."

I let out a startled laugh. "I'd be doing you a favor by taking some of your money? How much are we talking about here?"

"I was thinking around thirty thousand."

"What?" I say again, this time loudly.

"Maybe more?" he offers.

"This is a joke, right?"

"Not a joke. My parents left me more than the house when they died. I inherited a lot of money, Ruby, and the thing is . . . I can't use it. In fact, I don't use it. At all."

"What do you mean you can't use it?" This all sounds like a hoax. Too good to be true. I know these scams. Nobody just gives someone money for nothing. But Jared isn't a scammer. I know him too well at this point. He's so far from a con artist it's like comparing the brightness of the sun to the darkness of a black hole. "Why would you give your money to Paige?"

"Because it's not mine. Well, it is mine, but I don't want it. It would help me a lot if I could put it toward something good, like Paige. I already donate a bunch of the accrued interest but there's a lot left."

"I don't—"

"Don't answer now." He reaches out and puts a hand on my arm. "Promise you'll think about it. For Paige."

I can't do more than gape at him. Is he using my love for Paige against me? Just like my parents did? That doesn't make any sense. He's trying to give us something. Something I absolutely cannot accept.

A few months ago, I wouldn't have thought twice about taking money from some stranger who was willing to hand it over.

But now . . . Jared isn't a stranger.

I like him. I respect him. He cares about people. He cares about *me*.

He's like no one I've ever met.

I can't take his money and run. That would be . . . wrong.

In fact, everything I'm doing here is wrong.

I should tell him the truth. The whole truth. The thought

whispers through my mind, more tantalizing than last time.

I'm still staring at him when the sound of voices and laughter flits over us on the breeze.

"Did you hear that?" He tenses and moves closer to me, close enough that his arm brushes mine.

"I think I heard someone talking."

We wait in silence for a few more moments, and then the sound comes again. The breeze carries the sound past us, a laugh.

"Someone's over there," he whispers, leaning in even closer. His breath is a gentle tickle on my cheek and I suppress a shiver.

He grabs my hand and tugs me with him, creeping around the rocks. He stops and peers around the corner before jerking back against the rocks with me. "I think I saw someone. There was a flash of white over by the beach access."

"Should we go see?"

He nods, then peeks around the corner again. "Let's go."

My hand is still clasped in his. We run from behind the rocks to a large bush, where he stops again and tries to peer down the path.

"Do you see anyone?"

"No," he whispers.

The laughter reaches us on the wind again. "Someone's definitely down there."

We come out from behind the tree and Jared leads me down another winding, steep path that brings us closer to the ocean. This one isn't quite as sketchy as the last downhill route. There are stone stairs carved into the side of the mountain and a handrail to grab on to.

The moon moves behind a cloud and then it's too dark to see much, but the sound of voices is louder.

Jared halts on the steps and I nearly run into his back. I stop just in time and hang on to his waist.

"It sounds like kids maybe," he says.

"I can't see anything."

"Me either. Might have to turn on the light."

"What if they bolt?"

"Unless they have a boat, they have nowhere to go except toward us or down the beach. Either way they'll be in plain sight."

"Okay. Let's turn on the lights then."

We click on our flashlights and aim them toward the beach below. There's a shriek and I immediately wish we hadn't turned the lights on.

In the cone of light I get a flash of a big, hairy, white ass.

"Oh my god." I shut my eyes and lean my forehead against Jared's back. "I've seen that ass before." I laugh.

His shoulders shake in time with my own. "Hey, Paul," Jared calls out, "Sheila."

"Hey, Deputy. We were just, uh—"

"Why are you guys always following us?" Sheila's voice calls out over the sound of crashing waves.

I have to peek out from behind Jared to see what's happening. Paul is standing next to the circle of illumination from Jared's flashlight, his hands over his junk. I can't barely see Sheila, Jared is keeping her out of the direct light, but I can make out her glowing-white presence somewhere behind Paul.

"If you want to join us you just have to ask," Sheila adds. "We're going skinny-dipping."

"We'll have to decline, but thanks for the offer," Jared says.

"Have you guys seen anyone else out here tonight? Or any other night in the recent past?" I call out before hiding behind Jared's back again. I can't stand here and look at their naked bodies with a straight face.

"Not sure we would notice if there were," Paul answers.

"Thanks a lot. We'll be leaving now."

Jared turns toward me, chuckling as he nudges me back up the steps.

Mr. Newsome stops us before we make it very far. "You're not going to cite us for indecent exposure or anything?"

"Paul!" Sheila hisses.

"Nope," Jared calls over his shoulder.

"You're not going to make us leave?" Paul asks.

"It's fine. Just watch the undertow and don't leave any litter behind."

"Well ain't that something," Paul says before his voice is completely muffled by the ocean and wind as we walk away.

I manage to make it back to flat ground before collapsing on the grass and completely losing it. "Why do we always find them naked?"

Jared laughs, too. He sits down next to me, his flash-light pointed at the ground between us. "It's easier than you might think."

I lie back on the grass, the cool blades tickling my neck. "Apparently. How many times have you come across them while you were working?"

"At least half a dozen now." His teeth flash in the darkness.

"No way."

He lies back next to me, his head turned in my direction. "The worst time was when they broke into Dr. Pritchett's office."

"What were they doing in a doctor's office?"

"It's not something I like to remember, but to give you an idea, Sheila was the nurse."

"No!"

"Oh, yeah."

We stare at each other, sitting under the stars in the darkness for a few long, tense moments. His eyes drop to my lips and I wonder if he's going to kiss me here, under the stars.

I want it so badly. I remember the taste of him on my tongue and my mouth waters.

But then he turns away, breaking the moment. He pauses for a few long seconds, his back to me before he rolls to his feet.

He brushes his hands off on his pants before holding his hand out to help me up. When he speaks his voice is quiet, almost disappointed. "Come on. Let's go home."

12

___

$\mathcal{A}$ couple of days pass without incident. Paige and I fall into a routine with Jared. An entirely too comfortable routine.

I don't bring up going back to Tabby's, even though she's home, and no one else mentions it either.

There have been a few moments since the bluffs when I thought Jared wanted to kiss me, but something is holding him back. He always turns away or changes the subject. Even though I've been the one to halt things when they get too intense, his deliberate rejection still stings. I know he's doing it because he thinks it's what I want, but the more time I spend in his company, the more I'm not sure about . . . anything.

I installed a camera at the general store, and I've viewed a few hours of tapes here and there, but so far no glimpses of our parents or anyone familiar that might be connected to them.

I also don't get any more little love notes or calls from them, so . . . small mercies.

The napkin I found on the bluff isn't anything special, just a normal bar napkin from Ben's. I guess anyone could have left it out there or dropped it or something. It's weird though; those little cocktail skewers were also found at Mr. Godfrey's. Is there a connection? I don't know what it could be. Maybe the intruder goes to Ben's for drinks before breaking and entering? That wouldn't narrow down the suspect list very much. Everyone goes to Ben's.

It's a sunny Friday morning, with only a week before school ends and our great escape—a thought I have been avoiding with increasing frequency—when Jared gets a call.

"When? Last night?" he asks the person on the other end.

We're sitting at the table in the dining room, eating bagels and fruit. I watch him and listen to the one-sided conversation until he hangs up. "Another one?"

"Yep. Mrs. Newsome." He gulps his orange juice and stands.

I fold the newspaper I was reading and set it down. "I'm coming with you."

Sheila Newsome lives in a small house north of the boardwalk. Her lawn is small but well maintained with small, colorful pinwheels spinning in the flower beds near the porch. I also spy a couple of garden gnomes placed in compromising positions on our way to the front door.

The house itself is small—no more than two bedrooms, but it has ocean views from the windows in her living room.

"Did you hear any noises while you were sleeping?" Jared asks.

Today, she's much more dressed than the last time I saw her—thank the lord—in a long T-shirt and zebra-striped leggings. Jared and I sit on the couch, and she sits in a chair across from us.

"I heard the door shut and then it sounded like someone walking around in the kitchen. There's a few creaky boards in there. So I got up to see what it was, but no one was there."

"Was anyone else home with you?" I ask.

"No," she answers quickly. Too quickly.

"Mr. Newsome wasn't here?" I try again.

She presses her lips into a thin line. "I don't see how that's any of your business."

"Now, come on, Sheila," Jared cajoles. "You know we have to ask these questions. If he was here, he might have seen or heard something you didn't."

"Fine. He was here. But he slept through the whole thing. That man snores louder than a chainsaw in winter."

That doesn't make any sense to me, but whatever.

"What happened next?" Jared asks.

"After I couldn't find anyone in the kitchen, I went to check the front door, and it was unlocked."

"Are you sure you didn't forget to lock it the night before?" I ask.

She glares at me. "I didn't forget any such thing."

She doesn't seem to like me very much. Maybe I shouldn't ask any more questions.

"Plus, my plant was moved," she adds.

"Which plant is that?" Jared asks.

"The one in the front entry." She nods in the direction of the door and we both turn to look at a table with a small cactus in a colorful pot. "It's always right there, but when I woke up, someone had moved it to the floor."

"Did it seem like maybe someone had knocked it down, accidentally?" I ask.

"No." She shakes her head. "It wasn't spilled or anything, and it wasn't right next to the table, either. It was over by the wall." She points to the wall opposite the door.

"Were there any other objects moved around or anything at all that might be helpful?"

She shrugs. "I don't think so. Oh, there was an umbrella in the plant." She nods.

"An umbrella?"

"Not a real one. One of those little miniature ones, you know, like the kind they put in cocktails."

Cocktails. First the sword, then the napkin, now this. It has to be linked to Ben's somehow. But the umbrella . . .

My mind jumbles around with the information I have, trying to piece it together like a puzzle with pieces that don't quite fit.

Jared is still talking to Mrs. Newsome.

"Thank you for your time. Do you know where we

can find Paul right now?"

Her eyes dart from Jared to me and then back again. She chews on her bottom lip.

"Is he here?" Jared asks.

"Maybe."

"Sheila," Jared says, his tone warning.

"He can't come out right now." She gives us a slow grin. "He's been a bad boy."

I wince, visions of old Mr. Newsome tied up somewhere in the house dancing through my mind. It's not a pretty picture.

Jared shakes his head. "Well, have him call me when he has time, would you?"

She smiles and takes the card.

Back in the patrol car, I can't help but laugh. "They are something else."

"I know." He starts the car and pulls out of the small driveway. "But it's worked for them for almost thirty years."

"How long have they been 'separated'?" I make air quotes around the last word.

"I don't know exactly. Maybe five years. Paul bought a small cabin outside of town, but I don't think he's ever there."

I nod and we lapse into a comfortable silence. I'm still thinking about the possible connections between the incidents and Ben. I should say something to Jared; maybe he can help put the pieces together. But in order to keep up the pretense of Ruby, I don't want to say anything until I know more.

Jared drops me off at the shop, and I take the case file with me. "I want to go through your notes again," I say as an excuse.

What I really want to see are the dates.

Once he's gone, I go up to the office and peruse the file, searching for the dates of each incident. All of them —with the exception of the incident here at Ruby's— happened on Thursday nights.

The break-in here was a Tuesday. But it's the only anomaly, and it might be because the persons who broke in here were the parents, while the other incidents are connected.

Thursdays. Hmmm. Thursdays.

Mocktail night, Ben told us during trivia.

Are one or more of the old people who go to the mocktail night breaking into people's houses? Why? Are they getting drunk on the sly?

Even if they are, why would they then break in to people's houses and do . . . nothing? Except track in dirt and freak people out by cleaning their dishes or putting random items in the freezer.

I should talk to Ben to get more information. I call Tabby first.

"Hey," she answers.

"Hey, do you know where Ben is?"

"Nope. And it's awesome. I told him what I told you, you know, about how I'm not his little bitch, and he super stinks, and he can't make out with me anymore."

"You were never his little bitch."

"Close enough."

"What did he say when you told him?"

She huffs into the phone. "He doesn't believe me. He thinks I'm overreacting and everything will stay the same and I'm gonna let him stick his stupid tongue down my throat the next time we're at the bar, but Ruby, I'm telling you, it's not going to happen. Anyway, that was a couple days ago and I haven't even thought about him since," she says, her voice proud.

"That's great, Tabby."

"Well, maybe I've thought about him a little, but it was only because I was trying to find something to clean my toilet and I found his toothbrush and used that."

I laugh. "That's one way to get over someone."

"Yeah. So why do you need Ben?"

"It's for the case."

"Is he a suspect? Because I want to go to the jail and heckle him if he gets arrested."

"He's not a suspect," I say. "He might have some info we could use, though."

"Bummer. He's probably at work. They do inventory every Friday."

"I'll try him there. Thanks, Tabby. And Tabby?"

"Yeah?"

"You deserve someone who will treat you like a princess. I think he really does care about you, but he's gotten so used to being able to rely on you, too. Make him work for it, but if you really care about him, don't be afraid to give in. Once he's proven himself, of course."

She's quiet for a moment and then she sighs. "I know. Thanks, Ruby."

We hang up and then I dial the number for Ben's. He is there, but he's doing inventory, like Tabby said. He'll come by the shop when he's done.

I spend some time reviewing the tapes from the general store.

I have the file playing in fast forward, not really anticipating seeing anything of importance. But then something catches my eye. I stop the recording and rewind, then hit play, watching the scene more carefully.

The camera is facing the front checkout counter. The woman in line is the one who caught my eye. She looks like nearly everyone else in town, gray hair, old, and slightly hunched over, but she's wearing high heels.

And not just any high heels. Those are a top-of-the-line, eight-hundred-dollar pair of Jimmy Choos. Old people don't wear those shoes. They have bad hips and knees and wear orthopedic flats.

That's not an old lady. That's my mother.

I pause the tape and peer at it closer. She's wearing a wig. I press play and watch her fake an arthritic shuffle.

My heart thumps dully in my chest. I thought they were here, I knew they were, but part of me had hoped I was wrong.

Where have they been hiding?

A pounding downstairs derails my thoughts.

Shutting off the computer monitor, I hasten downstairs.

Ben's the one knocking. That was way faster than I thought it would be.

"Hey," he says when I open the door and let him into

the shop. "Is Tabby okay?" He pulls his baseball cap off his head, holding it in front of him.

Is that why he came straight over here? He's worried about Tabby? "She's fine. I called you about the case, actually."

His arms fall to the side, the ball cap in one hand. "Oh. Right. Yeah. That's what you said on the phone but I thought . . . whatever." He shakes his head. "How can I help?"

I tilt my head at him. His face is scruffier than normal, and he has gray smudges underneath his eyes. He looks like hell. I knew he would miss Tabby, but I wonder if he even realizes how much he needs her. And with that thought, an idea emerges.

I did want to help Tabby, after all.

"Come with me."

He follows me into the reading room, where I have him sit across from me.

"I need you to close your eyes," I tell him.

Poor guy is real confused. "What is this about?"

"Trust me."

He finally complies, his eyes falling shut, although his shoulders are still tense.

"Now I want you to relax." I keep my voice soothing and low. "Take a deep breath, hold it in. Now release the breath slowly." I perform the motions with him, letting him hear my own breathing to help him comply and relax himself. "Imagine all your worries leaving your body along with your breath." He relaxes even further. It doesn't take terribly long. If his tired eyes are any indication, he hasn't been sleeping well.

"Concentrate on the sound and the feel of the air moving in and out of your lungs."

When nearly all tension has left his body, I reach over and smack him upside the head.

"Hey!" He startles, his eyes flying open. "What was that for?"

"That was for Tabby. And for you. Stop being an idiot."

He opens his mouth to protest but then shuts it. "You don't understand." He frowns, his face the picture of misery.

Except I do. "You love her, and it scares you. You don't want to lose her and are willing to be just friends if it means having her in your life. Even though that's not what you really want."

His eyes widen. "How do you know?"

"Everyone knows, Ben."

"Everyone?" he whispers.

"Miss Viola knows and she's half blind and deaf."

"Does Tabby know?"

"No. She's almost as big an idiot as you are. But she's right to push you away. If you truly care about her, you need to let her know and stop screwing around."

"What do I do?"

"Talk to Tabby. Tell her how you feel."

"But what if she—"

"Don't make me smack you again," I interrupt. "You do love her, right?"

His gaze sharpens on mine, his jaw set. He swallows. "I always have."

"Then stop making this so difficult. You're hurting, she's hurting, you can fix this."

"Do you really think she's hurting?"

"You think she doesn't care about you?"

"I know she cares about me, but you've met Tabby. She's all bright and happy and perfect, and I'm . . . a bartender."

"That is so lame. You really think she cares about any of that?"

"She should."

"Maybe you should let her make her own choices."

He shakes his head and runs a frustrated hand through his hair. "Maybe you're right."

"Of course I am. You need to find a way to show her you care. Show her you're willing to try. Prove to her you're not the total jackass you've been for the last . . . however many years. You might not be perfect, but you can be perfect for her."

He nods at me and then his eyes fall to the table. A moment later, he nods again to himself and then his jawline firms. When he meets my eyes again, they are clear and determined.

Maybe something good will come out of this.

"Was this the real reason you called me?"

"No, just part of it. I also need to ask you about something else."

"What is it?"

"Mocktail night."

13

"So you're telling me you think some of our elderly townspeople are drinking nonalcoholic drinks and then breaking into people's homes?"

"Well, when you put it like that."

We're back at Jared's house. Paige invited Naomi over and they're swimming in the pool. Their laughter and splashing provides a happy accompaniment while Jared and I talk by the patio kitchen.

I try not to think about what happened in that same pool last week. Jared has been teaching me how to swim—not anything fancy or more than doggy paddling at this point—but every time I get in the water with him, it gets a little bit easier. I even bought a one-piece swimsuit that was on sale at the general store. We are working up to the point where I'll actually be able to get in and paddle around without his arms holding me, ready to catch me if I falter.

He's the hottest security blanket I've ever had.

"Listen," I say. "I have a feeling about this. Plus the break-ins are happening on Thursdays and there's been martini paraphernalia at two of the crime scenes."

"Yours didn't happen on a Thursday."

I bite my lip. I should have known he would remember. "But all the other ones did. And I talked to Ben."

"Here," he hands me the spatula, "watch this for a second." He turns to open the package of cheese on the counter. "What did Ben say?"

I stare at the burgers on the grill, not really sure what I'm supposed to be doing. "He said he hasn't seen anything stranger than usual at mocktail nights, but he did say he thought it was weird how they all act like they're really drinking when he knows they aren't. Maybe we should check it out."

"Fine." He turns back around and puts the cheese on the burgers. Once his hands are free, I immediately hand him back the spatula

He takes it with a knowing smile and shuts the lid on the grill. "When's the next mocktail night?"

I frown, contemplating his question. "It's not until next Thursday."

"You in a rush for some reason?"

"No. But . . ." We won't be here much longer after that. After next week's Thursday-night mocktails, we'll have two days. Paige's last day of school is Friday, they have a half day. Our plan is to sneak away that same night, after the dance.

That leaves a week and some change. That's it.

I'm still not sure where we're going, but I think it

might end up being as far as the rickety old car will take us. The anxiety is still keeping me awake at night.

"We've already been staying with you for over a week. I'm sure you want to get rid of us. Nobody likes houseguests who overstay their welcome, right?" I make a face.

"I don't know, I've been enjoying having someone live with me who's completely useless in the kitchen. Makes me feel needed and manly."

I laugh. "Oh yeah, so manly." I tug on his apron.

Troy got it for him as a gag gift. It has the curvy outline of a woman in a bikini on the front of it—sans head so it looks like it should be his body.

He sways toward me, and we have one of those moments where I think he's going to kiss me or hug me or something, but before he gets too close, he leans back and then glances over at the girls in the pool.

"Dinner's ready," he calls out.

I grab a platter from the counter to the side of the grill and hold it while he loads it up with food. The girls chatter and squeal as they exit the pool.

I focus on the sound, shoving down a huge dose of disappointment. I wanted him to kiss me. I still do. If the girls weren't watching, I would probably be throwing myself at him right now.

I carry the food to the table a few feet away. The girls help themselves to drinks from the mini fridge, and we all sit down to eat.

The girls chatter about the dance next weekend, how all of the high-school kids in the county are bussed into the same school, and this year it happens to be in Castle Cove. They also chat about how some boy asked Naomi to go with him and she turned him down.

Then Naomi asks, "Are you guys going to the swap meet Sunday?"

"What swap meet?" I ask.

Jared answers. "It's at the old fairgrounds north of town. Retailers from Castle Cove, Roseburg, and Trinity meet up for a big sale. There is a bunch of stuff, clothes, trinkets, anything you could imagine. We could all go together. You too, Naomi." He lifts his brows toward her.

Paige and Naomi exchange an excited glance. "Yes!" Paige says.

"I have to check with my grandma," Naomi says but she's grinning right along with Paige.

"Do either of you have dates for the dance?" I raise my eyebrows at them.

Paige rolls her eyes. "No way, all the boys at school are so gross."

Thank god for that.

Jared catches my relieved look and gives me a wink.

The girls keep the conversation going, and I pretend to listen while I think about the other item on my own agenda, one I haven't shared even with Paige.

The parents.

Once Ben left the shop earlier, I made some calls and a list of places they might be staying.

If I can find out where they are, maybe I can get ahead of them somehow—figure out what their plan is.

One of their biggest downfalls is how predictable

they are when it comes to certain things. Like, they won't stay anywhere that isn't ultra classy and high-end. They have a reputation to uphold, and well, they like to have the nicest things possible. Always. That significantly narrows down where they could be staying. It's possible they've rented a house, but there aren't many places for rent in little Castle Cove—Paige and I got lucky with Ruby's. More likely, they're staying at one of the hotels on the beach. There are two, one on the north side of Castle Cove and one a few miles south, outside of town limits.

I called both of the hotels and it only took a few attempts to figure out which hotel they were at. The Seaside Inn, in Castle Cove. They used the same alias they were using at the last place we stayed, which surprised me. The hotel didn't tell me which room they're in, they only offered to connect me. I hung up. Then again, maybe it's not so surprising. They're confident enough that I won't go after them and that if I try, I'll fail.

I'll have to show them otherwise.

Tomorrow.

The next day after Jared drops me off, I make my way to The Seaside Inn. It takes me a little over a half an hour to walk there.

It's a beautiful hotel, towering, white, and pristine. Every room on the backside has beach access. They also have a pool, a spa, and a French restaurant on the ground floor by the lobby.

People outside on the restaurant patio are drinking mimosas and enjoying the late-morning summer sunshine without a care in the world.

Must be nice.

I walk into the elegant front entrance. A few people stand in line at the check-in desk, so I wait my turn while covertly glancing around. There are high ceilings and sprawling windows with ocean views, and the floor has been polished so clean I can see my reflection.

No sign of my parents, not that I expected it to be that easy. I'm not sure what I'm going to say if I do find them. I'm not sure I want to find them at all. I just want to know where they are. I brought one of our extra spy cameras too. Even if I can't find their room number, I can leave a camera somewhere to catch their comings and goings.

Once it's my turn, I smile at the receptionist—a young, dark-haired guy in his late teens with a smart suit on. His nametag reads *Justin*.

"Hi." I give him my best and brightest smile. "I'm looking for a couple that's staying here, Mr. and Mrs. David Hampton?"

An inside joke of sorts. They always use aliases of famous con artists.

The kid types something into the computer and then his eyes lighten and meet mine. "Are you Charlotte?"

This is not good. "Ye-es?" I finally answer.

He nods and smiles. "Your aunt and uncle were expecting you. Super nice couple."

They must have tipped well. Does that mean they're coming off a big score?

"They checked out this morning, but they left something for you." He turns to get something from behind the counter. When he comes back around, he hands me a white envelope.

"Thanks."

"Have a nice day."

The outside of the envelope is blank. While I'm walking away from the counter, I tear it open.

Inside is a crisp, white piece of paper. It has the hotel logo at the top.

Nice try, it reads.

I groan in frustration.

How did they know?

14

———

Back at Ruby's, I pace in the office. They had to know I was coming. But how? Have they been watching us somehow?

I stalk to the window, then gaze down on the street.

Nothing.

I resume my pacing.

But what if . . .

I stop in the middle of the room and turn toward the phone.

It's an old-style handset. So old it even has a cord. I rush over to the desk, then stare down at it. I need to think rationally. If they did bug the phone, I don't want them to know I know.

Carefully, I pick up the handset and unscrew the bottom of the mouthpiece.

Sure enough, I find a bug. They bugged the phone. That's how they knew I'd found them. They heard my conversation when I called the hotel.

Racing downstairs, I check the phone in the kitchen. It's also bugged.

How did they get past the cameras?

Not that it matters. What matters is they've been listening in on the phone conversations I've been having. Granted, other than talking to vendors and taking the occasional customer call, or calling Paige at Jared's to make sure she got home from school, there's nothing much that I've given away that they couldn't have figured out on their own.

I walk back up to the office at a slower pace.

The good news is that I know about the bug, and I can use it to our advantage.

And with that thought in mind, a plan emerges.

On Sunday, we pick up Naomi and Jared drives us all the thirty minutes out of town, to the fields north of Castle Cove.

Paige and Naomi are more excited than I would have imagined. Who knew teenage girls could get so worked up over a swap meet?

Jared takes the top off of the Jeep so the breeze is in our hair. It's going to be a hot day. I wore a thin-strapped tank top and short-shorts that were in the stack of clothes Tabby gave me. The sun warms my bare shoulders while we drive, and Jared's occasional glance at my exposed legs warms the rest of me.

I can't hear the girls over the wind, but I see their

happy faces and catch wisps of their conversation in the back seat.

Jared and I are a bit more sheltered in the front seat because of the windshield.

I haven't told Paige about our parents. No need to worry her. I'm going to find a way to trick them, beat them at their own game so they can't find us on Friday night. I have an idea.

"I got a list of the people who've been attending the mocktail party from Ben," Jared tells me, jarring me from my thoughts. "I figured we could talk to a few of them, see if anyone has noticed anything suspicious the past few Thursdays. And you can feel them out."

I nod in agreement.

"Some of the people on the list we've already talked to, more than once. Like Mrs. Olsen."

No shock there.

"Stop talking about work and turn up the music!" Paige leans forward to yell at us in between the driver and passenger seats.

Jared complies and turns up the radio, which is playing some old country song I don't recognize, but Paige and Naomi are singing in the back seat.

The sun is warm on my face and I can't help but lean back and enjoy the moment while it lasts.

The swap meet is set up in a giant grassy field. Much like the other festivals I've been to around town, there are various booths selling wares and food, and they have games and other activities for kids. We park in a nearly full dirt lot. It takes a few minutes to find an empty spot.

Once we've parked, Paige asks if they can go searching on their own, so I hand her some money and tell her to meet us at the entrance in three hours. They take off almost immediately, giggling and chattering the entire time.

"I guess it's just us," Jared says.

We follow the girls, walking side by side through the parking lot. Close enough that our hands brush if I lean slightly to the left. "I guess so. Do you think you can handle it? We've been around each other a lot lately."

He grimaces. "Yeah, it's been a real struggle."

"I'm pretty needy."

He laughs.

We reach the entrance of the swap meet. Quite a few people are already meandering about, families, couples holding hands and perusing items at various booths, and some elderly people with walkers and fanny packs. The smell of fried food wafts through the air on the slight breeze.

"Are you hungry?" he asks.

I didn't think I was but whatever I'm getting a whiff of is making my mouth water, so I nod.

"They have the best taco truck. Come on." He grabs my hand, lacing his fingers through mine while we wind through the booths and people. It's not too crowded. He doesn't need to hold my hand and he doesn't need to wind his fingers through mine. This isn't the way friends hold hands. My heart flutters with the contact. He's been a little more distant lately. Our late-night swimming sessions have been nothing but platonic, which is what I wanted. Or thought I wanted. Is it fair of me to grab at what little happiness I can get, even if I know it will be over in a week and I'll be leaving Jared behind with no explanation? Is it fair to use him and let him discover later that it was all a lie?

It's not all a lie, though. Not the flip in my stomach when his hand tightens around mine, not the rush of my heart in my ears when his eyes drop to my mouth and definitely not the pang in my chest when I think about the future. Or lack thereof.

"They've got chicken, beef, or shrimp," Jared tells me.

We've stopped at the end of a line outside of the taco truck. Right. Food.

"Are you okay?"

I force myself to shake off my thoughts. "I'm good." I smile at him, and I mean it.

We order our tacos and find a seat at one of the many picnic tables lined up in the shade of a giant tent near the truck.

"After tacos, we have to play the swap meet game," Jared says.

"What game is that?" One of the carnival game booths?

"It's a challenge Troy and I made up. To find the worst, most tacky or bizarre or disgusting item for sale in this whole place."

I laugh. "How do we determine who wins?"

He shrugs. "We can have Naomi and Paige decide. But we can't tell them who picked what. I don't want you to have any sisterly advantage."

"And what does the winner get?"

"What do you want?"

That stumps me. I can't ask for him to cook dinner, he already does that almost every night. I can't ask him to teach me to swim, he's already doing that, too. Hell, he wants to fund Paige's college education. A topic that thankfully has not come up since the night at the bluffs.

Pretty much anything I want or need, Jared provides without me even having to ask. And he never wants anything in return.

"I don't know," I finally answer him. "What do you want?"

His eyes search mine before he responds. "A date."

"A date?" My brows lift. "With who?"

"With you. Who else?"

I stare at him, dumbfounded. "You want to go on a date with me?"

"That's what I said."

"Like a real date?"

"Is there any other kind?"

I've never been on a date.

"Well now I don't want to win." Immediately my face is on fire. I can't believe I admitted that much to him.

And what am I thinking? I can't date Jared.

His brows surge upward, and he can't suppress his grin. "It's a date then."

"But what about the game?"

"Winner gets to pick where our first date will be. We can go next weekend, if you're free?"

And immediately the happiness bubbling up inside

my chest is doused in a cold vat of ice water. We won't be here next weekend.

I force myself to smile and nod and then take a giant bite of one of my tacos so he hopefully doesn't notice my heart sinking.

I can't agree to a date, although it would appear that I just did.

"Hey guys." Troy plops down on the bench seat next to me. "Those look good."

Before I have a chance to say or do anything, Troy grabs a half-eaten taco off my plate and takes a giant bite.

"Dude," Jared says.

"I'll get you another one," Troy says through a mouth full of food. "I didn't eat a lot when I was sick."

"That's okay, I'm stuffed anyway." I push the paper plate in Troy's direction.

"Awesome." Troy takes another big bite, finishing off the whole thing. "I'm glad you guys are here. You can help me find a birthday present for Tabby."

"When's your birthday?" I ask.

"Three weeks. We have a tradition. Every year we use the swap meet to give each other the most bizarre present we can find. Last year I found this miniature toy rat in a box, and it has a button on the bottom and when you click it, it screeches like it's dying. It's so weird. I totally won. I've won for the last three years and I don't want to lose my streak."

"Well, you're in luck because we're searching for bizarre today," Jared says.

"That's the best game ever," Troy says.

"What did Tabby get you last year?"

"A baby doll formed out of used staples."

"Sounds dangerous."

"We definitely saved some poor kid from tetanus. And nightmares."

"Hey, Troy can help us determine who wins the bet. He can choose who picks out the worst item."

"And I can give that to Tabby for her birthday," Troy adds. "As long as it doesn't suck. Which it might, because no one can beat me when it comes to bizarre. Let's face it, I'm the champ. What's the bet?"

I watch Jared as he answers. "The winner gets to choose where we're going on our date."

Troy's brows lift. "A date, huh?" He jabs me with an elbow.

"Shut up Troy, or I'll hex you."

He presses a hand to his chest. "You wound me."

"Where's Tabby?"

"She's working the booth."

"Shouldn't you be helping her?" Jared asks.

"I was. I told her I had explosive diarrhea. She won't expect me back for a while."

I laugh. "You're gross."

"Hey, if it works . . . She's leaving in an hour anyway. You guys can meet me at our booth later with your chosen items. Choose wisely," he intones dramatically.

A few minutes later, Troy leaves us to find Eleanor—the library has a booth somewhere nearby.

Jared finishes his food and throws away the trash,

and then we meander through the meet, stopping at places that look like they have interesting items.

"So tell me," Jared says when we're perusing the shelves in a booth full of small painted figurines. "What's your favorite food?"

"Why do you want to know?"

"So I can figure out where to take you on our date when I win this competition."

There's a pang somewhere in the vicinity of my heart and I turn away, picking up a small porcelain clown. I show it to him with a grimace.

"Creepy," he agrees.

"Who says you're going to win?"

His answer is a grin. "I think the odds are in my favor."

"I like lots of different foods." I place the creepy clown back on the shelf gently. "I guess my favorite is Italian. Carbs and wine always sound good. What about you?"

"Cake."

I laugh. "Really?"

"I have a terrible sweet tooth."

You can't tell by looking at him. His lean and muscular frame is apparent even through his T-shirt.

He picks up a small figure. It's a porcelain clump of brown. "What is this?"

I eyeball it. "Poop?"

"This is a pretty good crappy present. Get it, crappy?"

"Ha ha, cheeseball. What's your favorite kind of cake?"

"German chocolate for sure. You?"

"Cheesecake."

"That's not real cake."

"It's called cheese*cake*, it's in the name. Of course it's real cake."

"If it has pie crust, it's not cake."

"Then why is it called cheesecake?"

"It's one of those weird word things, you know, like how tomatoes aren't vegetables, spiders aren't insects, and Batman isn't a real superhero."

"None of that makes any sense."

He leaves the porcelain poop behind and we head over into the next booth. This one has hats. Cowboy hats, sombreros, and baseball caps with various phrases and team logos. I pick up a shiny pink rhinestone cap and stick it on Jared's head.

He grins at me all goofy, making me laugh before I take it off his head and put it back on the rack.

"What's your favorite thing to do, you know, when you aren't taking care of Paige or working at the shop?" He picks up a cowboy hat and places it gently on my head.

"What's up with the third degree?"

He shrugs. "I don't know a lot about you, and I want to know more. You look cute in that," he adds with a smile. Then his head tilts at me and his gaze becomes a bit more focused. "Is it okay if I ask you questions?"

I duck my head so he can't see the smile forming on my face. "Yeah. It's okay. What was the question again?"

He smiles and takes the hat off my head, using the

opportunity to lean in closer. "What's your favorite thing to do?"

I turn away, fingering a floppy leather hat. It looks like something Indiana Jones would wear. What is my favorite thing to do? "I like to watch old movies and TV shows."

"*I Love Lucy.*"

I smile again. "You remember."

"Of course. What's your favorite movie?"

"It's so hard to pick. I think *Calamity Jane.*"

"I don't think I've seen that one."

"It's a musical. Pretty cheesy, but I think that's why I like it. Plus Doris Day is sort of a badass. Even when she's singing and dancing around and that terrible part where they make her all girly. What's your favorite movie?"

"*Tombstone.*"

"Ah. That makes sense. Law dog."

He grins. "That's me."

He continues asking me questions while we pretend to look at hats.

He covers everything, from my favorite color—dark blue, which I decide on a whim because it's the same as his eyes while they watch me—to the first boy I kissed.

"His name was John Smith. I was in seventh grade, and it was a dare," I tell him.

"John Smith, really? Are you making that up?"

I laugh. "I'm not, swear to god. True story."

I went to seventh grade for two months, long enough for the excitement of being the new kid in school to get me an invite to my first middle-school birthday party. We played spin the bottle and truth or dare, and I got to kiss my first boy. It was brief, awkward, and wet.

"What about you? When was your first kiss?" I ask. We leave the booth of hats and wander down the way, stepping around families with strollers and couples holding hands.

"First grade."

"You slut."

"I'll never forget Jana Fisher. I kissed her on the cheek and then she threw a clump of mud at my head."

I laugh. "You must have been a terrible kisser."

"I think maybe I've improved since then."

I wrinkle my nose. "Meh. Maybe a little."

"No one has thrown mud at me lately." He lifts his brows at me.

"Maybe there was nothing within reach to throw."

"Okay, I get it." He grins at me, putting his hands in his pockets. "You've told me about your first love. What about your last?"

I shake my head and sigh. "I have no story. I've never been in love."

"Really? Never ever?"

"Well, I mean, I've dated guys, I've just never . . ."

"Wanted to settle down?"

I nod. "We moved around a lot when I was growing up. I never really had time to form permanent attachments." I realize I have no idea if this is true for the real Ruby. Probably not.

I turn the tables on him before he can ask more. "What about you, ever had a grand love affair?"

"Not really. I thought I was in love once, but in hindsight, I think it was just infatuation."

It shouldn't bother me that he's had other girlfriends. Other girlfriends? What am I thinking? In a week, I'll be the girl he used to know. "What happened?" I am entirely too curious.

"I met a girl when I was in college. Sophia. We dated for a while and after graduation she wanted to move in together, but it wasn't the right time. Then I got a job as a police officer, which was a crazy schedule anyway. Then my parents died and . . ." He shrugs. "I moved back here. We tried to stay in touch, but our lives are too different. We're still friendly, but there's nothing there anymore. I don't really think there ever was."

We stop outside a booth full of clothing. They have a whole section devoted to cat shirts and, surprise surprise, Mrs. Olsen is sorting through the racks, stacking clothes on top of Miss Viola's wheelchair while Miss Viola snores away.

"Oh, Deputy, I'm so glad you're here," Mrs. Olsen says when she spots us entering the booth.

"Hey, Mrs. Olsen."

"What do you think about this shade of purple on me?" She holds the shirt up against her chest.

"It looks great," he says.

"Do you really think so? Will you come look at this?" She drags him across the booth to another stack of clothes, leaving me behind with Miss Viola, who's still sleeping. It's a little stuffy in the booth despite a fan blowing in the corner, so I try to move some of the clothes off of her lap. Don't want her to get a heat stroke in her sleep. The movement wakes her up and she clutches at my arm with one withered but surprisingly strong hand.

"Oh, it's you," she says.

"Hey Miss Viola," I say loudly.

"Are we done shopping yet?" she asks.

"I think Mrs. Olsen is still shopping for shirts."

"Who hurts?"

"Shirts," I yell. "Mrs. Olsen is looking for shirts."

Miss Viola frowns and waves a hand at me. "That old lady has enough of those damn cat clothes."

I let out a startled laugh.

"Would you stop talking trash behind my back?" Mrs. Olsen yells at us from the other side of the booth.

A few customers in line between us turn to see the commotion.

I don't like having so many eyes on me. Why are they staring? I wasn't the one yelling. When I glance down at Miss Viola, she's full-on sleeping, head back, mouth open.

There's no way. She's totally faking it.

I don't have time to test the theory because Jared is at my elbow, tugging me away. "We need to get out of here," he says under his breath. "She wants me to help her pick out lingerie."

I snort out a laugh, and I swear Miss Viola chuckles too, but then the sound turns into a snore.

Does this woman fake everything? The hearing and the sleeping? It's actually pretty clever. I wonder how much she overhears because people assume she's deaf and unconscious half the time.

We escape without having to see Mrs. Olsen's underthings, and the next booth we stop at is a treasure trove of odd items.

"Oh, yes. This is the winning booth, I can feel it," Jared says.

I spot a painting of dead-eyed children eating ice cream cones, staring out of the portrait like zombie babies. There's a spider-shaped wind chime that makes me shiver and a bunch of random trinkets and antique-looking toys.

"Check this out." Jared holds up a flowerpot. At first glance, it looks like a blooming red flower inside your basic clay pot, but when I get closer I can see it's not a real flower at all. It's not even fabric. Oh, no, this flower is made out of teeny tiny plastic penises, all melded together and then painted over to form the stem and petals.

"What is that?"

"Art?" He eyes it dubiously.

"You think that's art?"

"It could be making some sort of feminist statement. You know, because flowers are usually used to describe more, ah, female parts."

"That's a pretty good gift for Tabby." I purse my lips. Now I have to try and find something even better. "It's going to be hard to top."

We're running out of time. We've got to meet Naomi and Paige soon, so I've got to pick something at this booth or nothing at all. Finally, I settle on an odd item that's creepy, but not quite as cool as the penis flower. It's a toilet paper roll holder formed out of fake, plastic fingers. The fingers are all different sizes and shapes. Some even have nail polish.

"That thing is creeping me out," Jared says. "I'm not sure if I could wipe my ass with something I pulled from that."

We pay for the items and head out to find Tabby's booth.

It doesn't take long because there's a special section for the Castle Cove retailers.

We find Troy there making absolutely no attempt to help the people coming into the booth for the hardware store. He's sitting on one of the tables, swinging his legs and looking bored.

His expression brightens when he sees us enter the booth. "Check this out." He holds up a plastic package. It's a doll. A man-shaped doll. The packaging reads *Grow a Boyfriend.*

"What is that?" Jared asks.

"It's a man for Tabby. Now Mrs. Olsen will leave her alone." Troy laughs. "It's like sea monkeys, but it's a dude. You put water on it and it grows. You can also dry it out and reuse it." He grins. "Tabby will love it."

"Tabby is going to kill you," I say.

He nods. "Probably. What did you guys pick out?"

I show him my toilet paper holder made out of fingers, and Jared holds up his penis flower.

"The flower is pretty good. But not as good as mine.

You guys both suck. I win. I get to decide where your date is."

"That wasn't part of our agreement," Jared says. "In fact, you weren't even involved in our agreement."

"I think you guys should go to . . ." Troy continues as if Jared hadn't spoken. "Something boring. Jared likes boring," he tells me as an aside, as if Jared isn't standing right there. "Like a museum. Not a cool one, either, you should go to one of those weird ones that are trying to make a statement with things like dried bologna on the wall and mannequins dressed in trash."

"Is there something like that around here?" I ask.

"No," Troy says.

"Thanks, Troy, we're leaving now." Jared places a gentle hand on my back, guiding me out of the booth.

"Fine," Troy calls out. "But don't be a douche. Go somewhere nice, not that place with the peanut shells on the floor!"

We meet the girls at the entrance to the swap meet and they show us their purchases. Paige has a bright-green knee-length dress with spaghetti straps, and it's long enough that it doesn't seem like it will be too risqué when she puts it on. Naomi's dress is dark purple, strapless, and floor length. They're going to look like little grownups.

Then Jared takes us to dinner, and I have to smile at his choice: a low-key pizza place with hay and peanut shells on the floor. They have a small arcade the girls spend most of their time in.

They have such a blast that they both pass out in the back seat almost immediately.

"Today was fun," Jared says. He put the top of the Jeep back on for the dark drive home.

"I had a great time," I say, and I mean it.

The whole day was so wonderful.

"Next weekend will be better." The smile he throws in my direction is both sweet and hopeful and sends a dart of shame straight to my heart.

It won't be better. We'll be gone.

I don't want to ruin today. But I think I have to. I can't afford to be distracted by anything or anyone. Not with the parents on our tail and Paige to consider. I can't do anything that might risk her safety. There's nothing to stop them from just showing up and claiming her. They are her parents and I have nothing to stand on other than my word, which is obviously weak at best. None of this is fair to me or Paige.

And what about Jared? If the parents show up, he might be the one who has to turn Paige over. In the best-case scenario, we leave and never see him again. I can't possibly go through the next week, playing along and then . . . just disappear. Wouldn't that be worse than letting him down gently? Before it goes further?

I don't know what I was thinking, letting myself get caught up in the fantasy of today.

How can I fix this now without seeming like a complete nut job?

"I might need a rain check on the date," I say, thinking quickly.

"A rain check?"

"I forgot I told Paige I would take her on a trip. Only for a week, up the coast, to celebrate the end of the school year."

He's silent, absorbing the poorly told lie about as well as I delivered it.

"I'm sorry . . . I don't know how I could have forgotten," I add.

"It's fine." He sends another smile in my direction, but this time it's bleak.

He knows I'm lying as surely as I know I've ruined everything.

The rest of the night is quiet. We drop Naomi off at home and then head to Jared's. Paige goes to bed.

I wait by the pool for Jared, but he doesn't show.

After thirty minutes sitting on a lounge chair alone, staring up at the stars, I head to bed.

It's for the best, I know.

15

onday morning, Jared's up and making breakfast like normal, and it's like nothing has changed.

As if the day at the swap meet and the night that I ruined everything never even happened.

It should make me happy. I don't have to worry about Jared nursing some kind of broken heart—as if I could inspire something as banal as a broken heart anyway—but then why can I hardly eat? The pancakes that normally taste heavenly are like lumps of dough in my stomach.

At least I have the case to distract me.

The first place we stop around midmorning is Judge Ramsey's house.

According to Jared, Judge Ramsey is semiretired. He still presides over cases in Castle Cove in the summer when he's here and when they have too many cases, which is rare. He and his wife live in a cute bungalow with a white picket fence north of the town proper and spend most of their time golfing at the country club and travelling to Arizona in the winter, where their son lives with his family.

When we arrive on their doorstep, the Ramseys immediately invite us in for brunch on the patio, which we can't refuse when I see that Mrs. Ramsey has made a giant lattice-topped apple pie.

"I didn't know pie was served at brunch."

"We're retired," Mrs. Ramsey says with a tinkling laugh. "We do what we want."

Mrs. Ramsey's white curls lay close to her head, like a flapper haircut, and she has an infectious laugh.

Judge Ramsey has white hair trimmed close on the side and slighter longer up top. He has a neatly trimmed moustache and wire-rimmed glasses.

Brunch is chicken and waffles. I've never had the combination, and it's delicious—sweet and salty and perfect with the pie. We don't ask any questions about the mocktail party while we're eating. It would be rude when they're feeding us and talking about more mundane things like their kids, the weather, and cases Jared and Judge Ramsey worked on together. When the food has been demolished, including the pie, the conversation turns.

"Do either of you young people play chess?" Judge Ramsey asks.

"I do," I say. "Not very well, though."

"Well, then I insist you stay a little longer and play a game with me. Mrs. Ramsey isn't a big fan of chess."

"Okay," I agree.

Jared turns to Mrs. Ramsey. "You mentioned you needed to move some items from the back shed. I can help you while they're playing."

"That would be wonderful," Mrs. Ramsey says.

She made overtures while she was serving the apple pie that she needed help and didn't want Mr. Ramsey hurting his bum knee.

Jared and I exchange a glance, silently agreeing to ask our questions about the case when we have them separated.

It's weird how we know what each other is thinking with no more than a glance or a nod. Paige and I are the same, but I've never had anyone else in that bubble before.

"So you and Mrs. Ramsey go to mocktail nights at the senior center?" I ask while Mr. Ramsey is setting up the board.

"Yes. It's our date night. It's an excuse for Mrs. Ramsey to dress up. We love to people watch."

"Do you ever see any people doing anything weird or unusual?"

He thinks about that while I move my rook. "Not really. Nothing more than usual. Although, I did see Miss Viola and Mr. Godfrey arguing one night, which was strange."

"Why was it strange?"

"Well, Mr. Godfrey wasn't speaking terribly loud and she didn't seem to have any problems hearing him at all."

I nod, considering the information. I'm not the only fraud in town. "That is interesting. Anything else? Did you ever see anything odd or out of place when you were driving home?"

He shrugs. "Not really."

We play in silence for a few minutes while we both consider the board and I consider what else to ask.

"You know, we had a similar situation here years ago," the judge says.

"What do you mean?"

"When I was in school, they had some senior prank incident and some kids got caught. Multiple houses were broken into. Nothing was taken though. They did random pranks like tying up sweater sleeves."

That sounds familiar. "When was this?"

He shrugs. "A long time ago. Maybe in the sixties." He frowns and thinks for a minute but eventually shakes his head. "Jared will probably have more luck getting information out of Mrs. Ramsey," the judge tells me with a wink.

I shrug. I suppose it was too much to hope that our little divide and conquer tactic wouldn't go unnoticed by Judge Ramsey.

"She pays more attention at those functions," he continues. "The truth is, I spend a majority of my time watching her while she does a majority of the people watching." He chuckles.

"You have been together for a long time."

"We met when we were eleven years old," the judge tells me, moving his rook on the board. "My mother told me it would never work because I was a Lutheran and she was a Catholic and back then, that was a big deal."

"It must not have been *that* big of a deal." I move my knight.

"It wasn't." He smiles at me over the rim of his glasses. "I converted."

"How long have you been married?"

"Almost sixty years."

"Wow, that's a long time."

We make a few moves in silence before he peers at me again. "Do you have a fella?"

Of course, that makes me think of Jared. "No." I move my king.

"You took a moment to answer. Is there someone special you're thinking about?" His eyes are twinkling.

"No. Yes. Well, maybe. I don't know. It's complicated."

"As someone who's lived many years on this planet, let me let you in on a little secret. It's only ever as complicated as you want to make it. It can be very simple."

Ah, let's see, so the simple version of my life is that I'm a former con artist; I've *technically* kidnapped my sister; I'm on the run from my embezzling parents while pretending to be someone I'm not; I'm staying with the local deputy who wants to be my boyfriend even though he doesn't know my real name; and the person I'm impersonating is going to be back in a couple short months and blow my cover. In the meantime, my parents are closing in and I need to leave town immediately. So simple.

"I don't know," I say. "It doesn't feel simple."

"Do you like him?"

The chessboard in front of me blurs as I probe my emotions on the matter. It's a simple *answer*, at least. "Yes." I move in on his king. "Check."

"Then nothing else really matters now, does it?"

I wish that were true.

"Let me put it another way," he says. "As you get closer to the end of your life, everything speeds up until you're holding a thread in one hand that's dwindling to nothing and another hand full of regrets. You can't change the past, and you can't predict the future. You may not like the choices you have in front of you, but you have choices. If you have a chance at happiness now, no matter how fleeting it might be, you should grab on to it with both hands before you're left with nothing. Even bad choices are better than none."

He smiles and moves his queen. "Check mate."

As Jared and I leave the Ramseys', I can't stop thinking about what the judge said. Should I grab on to what I want, even if it means more heartache in the future? Am I wasting valuable time pushing Jared away? Should I "live in the now," so to speak, if only to have memories when I'm long gone and he hates me for all my lies and deceptions?

The clock is ticking.

When we hop in Jared's Jeep, I force myself back to the case at hand. "Did you get any good information out of Mrs. Ramsey?"

"Not really, although she does think there might be more than cranberry juice in some of the mocktails that are being consumed."

"The judge mentioned something about this same type of incident happening in the 1960s. A senior prank thing, or something."

"Really?"

"Yeah. I wonder if some of our elderly folks are recreating old times. Would they have information at the station going back that far?"

He nods. "Probably in the archives. Do you think it's worth pulling up?"

"You have any better ideas?"

A short drive later, we're back at the station. The basement archives are dark and dusty. It smells like stale coffee and old paper. Most of the space is comprised of row after row of boxes with case files dating back to the early 1900s. The dim, flickering lights run on motion sensors and only click on when we walk down the aisles.

I shiver. "This place is like a horror movie."

"It's not fun coming down here alone. Especially if Troy is anywhere in the building. He likes to scream randomly down the stairs to freak people out."

"That sounds like him."

"Here's the boxes from the 1960s." Jared stops in the middle of one of the aisles. He pulls a box from the shelf and hands it to me. "We can take a few at a time over to the side room over there." He gestures to a small room with better lighting and a long table. A wide window overlooks the storage area, and there are no windows to the outside world. It's like working in a cave.

I nod, take the box, and head in that direction. The room is sparsely furnished. Just one table, a few chairs and a computer in the corner that is bigger than a microwave and probably hasn't been used since 1986.

I set the box on the table and open it up, riffling through the contents before pulling out the first stack of files.

Jared brings in his own box and we spend the next couple of hours going through old case files, only stopping to go to the bathroom and when Jared calls in some sandwiches for lunch.

It takes a while, but eventually we find something.

"Here." I hold up an old newspaper clipping, thin and fragile with age. "This says a few teens were held for questioning about a series of pranks that happened in 1962. They mention a secret club called the Knights and Ladies of the Red Baron."

Jared rolls his chair over next to me and peers at the article over my shoulder while I skim it.

"There was some sort of ritualistic rite of passage that the teens had to do in order to get into the club. One of them was caught trying to complete the fourth and final step, which was walking the plank at the Castle Cove ruins. Walking the plank?" I turn my head toward him.

"Oh, yeah. That was something we did, too. There's this old, thick, wooden board up at the castle set between the two columns that are still standing."

I nod, remembering our night out at the bluffs.

He continues, "Walking the plank is just walking across it without falling to your death."

"Seriously?"

He turns his head toward me and my breath catches in my throat at his nearness. His lips can't be more than a few inches from mine.

"Yeah." His eyes flicker down to my mouth. "But it's not dangerous when the tide is in. There's enough water that if you fell, you'd just have to swim to the shore. Plus, you know how it is when you're young and reckless." He pulls back from me, sliding back in his chair a couple of feet. "Does it say anything about the first three steps?"

He's looking away from me and my eyes are drawn to his strong jawline, his neck, his shoulders. I want to drag my lips over all those things.

But now his gaze is on me and the glint in his eyes is telling me he's all too aware of his effect on me.

I clear my throat and force my attention back to the article in front of me, gently turning to the next page. I pause on the picture accompanying the article. "No. But it does mention a former prominent member. This article was printed after she left the club, but she was active when she went to Castle Cove High."

"Who?"

I turn the black-and-white picture toward him. The woman has dark hair instead of white hair, and significantly fewer wrinkles, but she's wearing a sweater with a cat on it, and I would recognize her determined expression anywhere.

"Mrs. Olsen."

16

Jared makes some phone calls to track down our suspect. Mrs. Olsen is volunteering at the nursing home.

"What can you tell us about the Knights and Ladies of the Red Baron?" Jared asks.

We're outside of the activities room at the nursing home, where they have a guest teaching the residents how to salsa.

The pulsing music beats through the door into the hallway while we question Mrs. Olsen. She's wearing a tight-fitting, bright-yellow leotard covered in pink cats and a colorful skirt that flares around her hips. I wouldn't be caught dead in that getup but for some reason, on Mrs. Olsen, it almost looks normal.

"Did you say the Red Baron?" Mrs. Olsen laughs. "That brings back some memories."

"You were a member?" I ask.

"Me? I was the president."

Jared and I exchange a glance.

"What were the first three tasks that had to be completed to get into the club?" I ask.

"Oh, I can't tell you that."

"Why not?" Jared asks.

"I've been sworn to secrecy."

Jared sighs and rubs the back of his head. "Mrs. Olsen, this is in regards to an ongoing case. If you don't cooperate, you could be charged for impeding an investigation."

"That is bull honkey." She slaps him gently on the shoulder and laughs. "You wouldn't arrest me, Jared, I've changed your diapers."

He presses his lips together and I can't tell if he's embarrassed or holding back laughter. "That was a long time ago, Mrs. Olsen, and I would really appreciate your assistance on this case."

"I don't break my promises, young man. But maybe I can tell you about someone who wasn't sworn to secrecy like I was. He was a member sometime after me."

"That would be helpful," he says.

She looks at me and then Jared, clearly enjoying this whole conversation a little too much, if the sly grin on her face and twinkle in her eyes are any indication.

"Mr. James Bingel."

I can't imagine Mr. Bingel being a part of something like this, but Mrs. Olsen has no reason to lie, since she knows we'll be questioning him.

Mr. Bingel is at home when we stop by. He's helping the boys with their homework. He brings us to see them before we get down to business. They're sitting at a small circular table in the kitchen.

"Ruby!" Gary runs up and throws his arms around me. "Where have you been?" he asks, his little eyebrows drawn together.

"Paige and I have been staying with Jared for a little bit."

"Are you going to marry him?"

"Ha ha . . . haaa," the laughter leaves my mouth forced and stilted, my face heating with embarrassment. I don't look back at Jared. I can't. "We aren't getting married," I tell Gary. "We're here to talk to Mr. Bingel if it's okay with you guys."

We leave them in the kitchen with their work, and Mr. Bingel takes us into his study.

"How can I help you today?"

"We have some questions about a secret society you were a member of back in the day," Jared says.

At Mr. Bingel's confused expression, I offer, "The Knights and Ladies of the Red Baron?"

"Oh, yes." He chuckles. "That was fun."

"Do you remember if there were any tasks or steps you had to take to enter the society?"

"Well let's see now. I remember we had to walk the plank at the end." He squints his eyes, thinking. "That was the weirdest part. The walking of the plank could only be performed under the full moon. And you had to be in your birthday suit." His brows lift and he nods at us. "They still do that, I think, but now it's more of a dare and they wear their clothes. But back in the day . . ." His lips purse while he thinks. "There were some kind of pranks, moving things around people's houses, toilet-papering a yard, breaking chalk in the classrooms, that sort of thing."

Bingo.

I glance over at Jared and find him watching me. We smile and then turn back toward Mr. Bingel.

"Did you have to break into people's houses to perform these pranks?" I ask.

"Of course not. No one locked their doors back then. Not until the pranks became more widespread, at least. Once people started locking up at night, we moved on to targeting friends or family, people we already had keys for. We never did anything illegal. Just harmless jokes."

"How did you pick the people you would target?" Jared asks.

Mr. Bingel shrugs, pushing his glasses up on his nose to peer at Jared. "I don't really remember. As I said, they were always friends or family of people already in the club. That way we had a way in."

"Have you heard anything about the incidents recently, like at Ruby's?"

Mr. Bingel purses his lips. "You think these recent crimes are connected to something that happened fifty years ago?"

"We don't know." Jared says.

"I guess you could be onto something. The club disbanded right after I graduated. There were quite a few people who didn't get an invitation, and they were always rather bitter about it. It wouldn't surprise me if they resurrected the old ways just for fun."

"Do you know of anyone still around who might want to recreate old times?"

He shrugs. "I barely remember what I ate for dinner last night."

"What if we give you a list of names? Do you think you could point out anyone connected to the club?"

"I could try."

Jared pulls our list of the people who've attended the mocktail parties out of his pocket. He hands it over to Mr. Bingel with his pen. "If you could make a check next to the ones you think that might been in or wanted to be in the club."

Jared and I wait in silence while Mr. Bingel hems and haws and makes some marks on the paper.

"There." He hands the paper back. "I can't guarantee that's accurate, but it's to the best of my knowledge."

Jared stands and I follow. "Thank you for your help," he says.

We say goodbye to the boys and then head out to the patrol car.

"Well," I tell Jared, "I think we should see if our victims have given out any spare keys."

He makes the calls from the patrol car.

"Only Paige and I have a spare," I tell him about our house keys.

And the real Ruby. And her accountant. But that's it, and neither of them could be the culprit.

As Jared calls each victim, he tells me every time he

hangs up who has a spare key for each household. And every time, it's the same name.

"Mrs. Olsen," he says when he hangs up with Sheila Newsome.

"We keep coming back to her, don't we?"

"I guess we're going back to the nursing home."

Salsa class is over and Mrs. Olsen is in the front office helping with files, still in her leotard and skirt.

"Did Mr. Bingel tell you guys what you needed to know?" She picks up a file folder and slides it into a drawer.

"Actually he did," Jared says. "And we have another question for you."

"Go ahead."

"Why didn't you ever mention that you have a spare key to nearly every house that was broken into?"

Her head tilts. "But I don't."

"Everyone that's had a break-in, except Ruby, has given you a spare key to their house at one time or another."

"Well, they did, but I don't have them anymore." She turns her back to us, searching through some of the files. Or pretending to.

"What happened to them?" I ask.

"Hmmm? Oh, I stored the keys in the safest place I could think of, but then they got stolen."

"Stolen? When?"

"I'm not really sure . . ." She sidesteps away, down a couple rows of cabinets.

"Where were you keeping them?" Jared asks.

She fidgets with her multicolored skirt and finally faces us. "I was keeping them with Miss Viola. You see, she has these little pockets on her wheelchair she never uses."

I groan. This sounds so familiar. Miss Viola also had all the bags from the old Greek restaurant that were used the last time I helped with an investigation. The boys swiped them while Miss Viola was sleeping.

"Miss Viola's wheelchair probably isn't the best place to keep things. She's not exactly a good sentinel," I say.

"When was the last time you saw the keys?" Jared asks.

"I housesat for the Newsomes when they went on one of those cruises to Mexico. I've never gone on a cruise. I've heard people get food sickness, you know, and then the motion sickness and there are pirates—"

"Mrs. Olsen, please answer the question."

"Right, well that was about six months ago."

"So sometime in the last six months," I repeat. That doesn't give us anything to go on. "What did the keys look like? Did they have any identifying marks?"

Now Mrs. Olsen looks embarrassed. "They all kind of looked the same, and I have a really bad memory."

Jared's eyes fall shut and he groans. "Please don't tell me..."

"I wrote their names on them," she says with a small, guilty smile.

17

———

"That was a giant dead end," Jared says.

We're back at his house. Paige is doing homework and we're in the kitchen discussing the case after cleaning up after dinner.

"At least now we know how someone is getting into their houses," I say. "They took the keys right off Miss V's wheelchair. And it's got to be either someone that was in the Red Baron club or someone who tried to get in. Where's Mr. Bingel's list?"

We have a bunch of stuff spread out on the island in the kitchen. The map showing the locations of the incidents, some pictures of the items left behind and damage occurring during the pranks, witness statements, and Jared's notes from our interviews.

He pulls the list from his notebook and sets it in front of me.

"A lot of correlation here," I say.

He moves around the island and stands behind me, peering over my shoulder so he can see. He sighs. "Yep."

"It's got to be someone who goes to the mocktail party night."

"We're back to that, huh?"

"Well. We know now what we need to do."

He nods. "We need a plan for mocktail night."

We make a list of potential suspects, using the data we have. There are a few people we discount immediately—mostly because they're either wheelchair- or walker-bound and there's no way they could be slipping in and out of people's houses undetected. What we're left with is Mrs. Olsen, Mrs. Hale, and nearly a dozen other geriatrics whose names I recognize but haven't spent much time with. There are too many people for just the two of us to keep track of. Maybe we can have someone stake out the bar area to make sure no one is spiking the punch. And someone else set up outside the senior center to track our suspects as they leave.

"We need reinforcements," Jared says.

"Let's call in the troops."

The next night, Troy and Tabby come over for dinner. Ben couldn't make it because of work, or he couldn't face Tabby, or maybe a combination of both.

"We need new clothes," Tabby tells me over drinks before dinner.

We're reclining on the padded loungers in our bathing suits while Troy and Jared cook dinner.

Paige swims around in the pool, some new goggles Jared got her making her eyes buggy.

It didn't take long to hash out the details for mocktail night. Tabby will help Ben keep an eye on the bar to make sure no one is trying to inebriate the elders. Troy and Jared divvyed up the list of suspects to keep an eye on and decided to have Anderson patrol the area around the senior center that night. And me? I will be trying to get a read on anything out of the ordinary. With my abilities. You know, the nonexistent ones.

"Why do we need new clothes?" I ask her.

She looks at me over the rim of her giant black sunglasses. "For the party. Everyone gets dressed up. Do you have any prom dresses?"

She knows that I don't. "Um. No."

"Exactly. It will be so much fun, we can go to Roseburg on Thursday and get lunch and try on all the dresses. Maybe get our hair done before the party."

"I don't know, Tabby." It seems wasteful. I've gotten a couple small checks from the sheriff's office, and I've made a bit more off of readings that I stuffed into my hidey-hole, but we'll probably still need more when we leave.

"You should totally go," Paige chimes in. She's hanging on to the side of the pool, listening to our conversation. "You never get to do that kind of stuff." She gives me a meaningful look that says, *and you probably won't ever again.*

"Maybe." I can always return the clothes later.

Tabby smacks my leg with her hand. "So then it's settled, I'll pick you up Thursday morning at nine. Jared!" she yells suddenly.

He's over at the grill with Troy and he turns toward us, his brow furrowed.

"I'm stealing Ruby on Thursday. You don't need her, right?"

He shrugs and continues whatever he was saying to Troy.

"We are going to have so much fun." She leans back in the lounge chair next to me and lets out a contented sigh. "This backyard is to die for. We should have weekly dinner here instead of my little place."

"You talk like you haven't been here before."

"Because I haven't, not in a couple of years."

I turn my head toward her, shading the sun from my face. "What? No way."

"Way. After Jared's parents died, he didn't invite anyone over. Not until you." She bats her eyes and holds her hands against her face coyly.

I laugh and smack her hands down. "That's . . . super weird."

"Not really. He was sad. He wanted to be alone most of the time and it was hard having people here. His parents had parties and stuff all the time, too many memories. But now he's not so sad and he's more social."

"He doesn't really talk about his parents much." I look over at the grill where he's standing with Troy. He made Troy wear the apron with the curvy figure on it, so he's in his swim trunks and a T-shirt. He makes the simplest things look so good.

"Now let's talk about what we're going to buy on

Thursday. We should get you a yellow dress. You are totally a spring."

After Tabby and Troy leave, I decide it's time to show Paige my new secret.

Jared and I are sitting on the patio talking, and Paige has been in the pool—again. After we ate she wanted to go right back in.

"There's something I want to show you," I tell her.

She stops doggy paddling around the shallow end and stands as I head for the steps leading down into the pool. "What are you doing?"

"Watch."

Jared stays on the patio chair, watching with a small smile while I step into the pool without panicking and then crouch down—because it is pretty shallow—and doggy paddle my way over to where Paige is.

It's not the most impressive of moves. I mean, I could stand at any time so the risk of drowning in the shallow end with multiple onlookers might not be an extraordinary feat of . . . well, anything, but Paige's reaction is absolutely worth every second.

She shrieks. "You can swim!"

I paddle closer to her and she tackles me.

Laughter and Paige's slight weight push me under and make a bit of water go up my nose. But not for long. I stand up, snorting-slash-laughing while Paige hangs off me like a spider monkey.

"I can't believe it!"

"Jared has been teaching me."

"He has?" She glances his way.

"Yeah. I wanted to surprise you."

"Best surprise ever! Can we play Marco Polo until bedtime?"

"Sure, but I'm not a pro yet so go easy on me."

We spend the next hour swimming and splashing and playing together, like we have no other worries.

It's one of the best nights of my life.

And then it's bedtime.

Once we shower and get ready for bed and Jared is safely ensconced in his room, I sneak over to Paige's bedroom to finalize our plans.

"You worry too much. I got it down."

We already set everything in motion earlier in the week. When I was at Ruby's one afternoon, I called Paige like normal to make sure she was home and doing her homework, and then we laid the first set of our plans: misdirection.

We talked about the dance and how Paige would stay the night with Naomi afterward. I told her I would pick her up on Sunday morning, early, with our bags packed and leave town from there.

None of that is actually going to happen, but it's what we want our parents to think is going to happen.

It's a solid plan, but I'm still worried.

"I promise I'll be careful and keep an eye out," she says.

"Fine. I know, you'll be fine." I let out a sigh and slump next to her on the bed. "It's almost over."

"Yep," she says.

If for any reason one of us doesn't make it to the school after the dance, we're going to rendezvous at Jared's. He's the safe spot.

My safe spot. I know if anything happens to me before Sunday, he'll take care of Paige. And really, that's all that matters.

18

———

*T*hursday morning, Tabby shows up with coffee right at nine.

Paige is in school, Jared at work.

The drive to Roseburg is interesting. Tabby makes me listen to Christopher Cross and Earth, Wind & Fire the entire drive.

"This is not the music I pictured you listening to," I say when she's done belting out "Sailing."

"I am full of surprises."

Once we reach downtown Roseburg, she parks in a public lot and we walk along the bustling main street. It's quaint with an old-timey vibe and lined with boutiques and shops.

The first store we stop in has a bunch of dresses, most of which are dark with velvety fabrics.

"Hell, no," I say.

"Oh come on, Ruby, it's fun. What size are you?"

"I don't know, medium?"

"I mean dress size."

"I've never really had to buy a dress like this," I admit.

My parents dressed up all the time, but I was never allowed to go with them to their fancy dinners. They always used me for the more menial tasks. The only time I was allowed to attend anything swanky, it was suited up as the waitstaff.

"You never went to prom? Or were a bridesmaid?"

I never really went anywhere. I stopped going to high school at fifteen—unless my parents wanted me to for show or to get close to the kid of one of their marks. I never had any friends who would have asked me to be in their wedding.

"No. Prom wasn't really my thing," I hedge.

"Well here." She grabs a dress off the rack and holds it up to me. "This looks like it might work. Hold this." And then she begins stacking dresses. Some she keeps, and some she flings in my direction.

The dressing room is a wide, circular space where she insists I show her every single dress I try on.

"There is no way I'm wearing any of these." I've put on a slinky black dress that's too long in the sleeves.

Tabby laughs. "You look like you belong in a cemetery."

"All I need is dark makeup and a black wig. I vant to vear somethink that vill make people veddy veddy scared ov me," I intone.

Tabby snorts out a laugh.

Then I take note of her outfit. "What is that thing?"

"These clothes are crazy." She's wearing a short

yellow dress with puffy lace sleeves. She flaps her arms so the sleeves flutter up and down, then shuts the dressing room door to change. "But isn't this fun?"

It is fun.

I shut my own door to change into my clothes and a wave of sadness washes over me. I wish we didn't have to leave.

Tabby drags me to another store, this time not just for fun. We actually find a few decent dresses.

"This one." She holds up a slinky, light-blue, strapless dress.

I finger the soft fabric. "The color is really pretty."

"It will look amazing on you. Here, go try it on."

"What are you getting?"

She holds up a much shorter, bloodred dress with spaghetti straps. It looks like it could fit a baby.

"Is that for Paige?" I tease. "Because I think that's too small even for her."

"Ha ha. I'm want to make Ben go crazy."

"I think that will do it."

After dress shopping, we stop at a little cantina a few blocks away.

"The margaritas here are to die for," Tabby tells me, holding open the door to the restaurant.

It takes a few seconds for my eyes to adjust in the dimly lit interior. There's a family in line ahead of us, putting in their names for a table.

"How many?" the host asks when it's our turn.

Shit.

He's a young, dark-haired guy in his late teens. The last time I saw him, he was wearing a smart suit. This time, he's in khakis and a polo shirt emblazoned with the cantina's logo, but I recognize him regardless. His nametag reads *Justin*. What are the odds? And why on earth does he have another job an hour away from Castle Cove?

The moment recognition washes over his features, my stomach drops.

"Hey," he says.

"We have two in our party," I rush. If he's working multiple jobs, he probably sees all kinds of people all the time. He probably won't remember—

"It's Charlotte, right?" He's already making a note in a seating list.

"Charlotte?" Tabby asks from behind me. "Who's that?"

"Oh, that's my . . . middle name." Only a slight delay gives me away. Here it is, the moment of ugly truth. First the confusion, then the anger, then the throwing things at me. There's a handy tub of dinner mints on the host stand I'm sure will make excellent ammunition—

"Ruby . . . Charlotte?" Her nose scrunches up. "That's the worst name combo ever. What were your parents thinking? "

But Tabby isn't suspicious. She isn't looking for tells or reasons to doubt my word. Because I'm her friend. I'm her lying, kidnapping, thieving friend. Is that relief or regret draining the blood from my head?

"It's a family thing." I shrug and turn to Justin. "We have two in our party," I repeat. Deep breath in, deep breath out. Just get us to a damn table, Justin.

Tabby smiles at Justin, then at me. "How do you guys know each other then?"

Double shit.

But before I can come up with an answer to derail this line of inquiry—or fake a seizure, or shout, "Look, Elvis!"—ever-helpful Justin answers for me. "We met at my other job at The Seaside Inn." He bends over to pull menus and napkins from a cupboard under the counter.

"The Seaside Inn is pretty far from here," I say.

"My parents own both properties. I normally don't come all the way out to Roseburg, but someone had an emergency and they needed me to cover a shift." He shrugs.

Of course.

Tabby lifts a brow at me.

She's going to ask why I was at the Seaside.

Think, dammit. This used to be so easy. Why can't I think?

"Right this way," Justin says.

We follow him through the restaurant to a booth, at which point he lets us know our server will be right with us before thankfully departing.

Tabby grabs one of the menus. "So what were you doing at The Seaside Inn? Illicit rendezvous? Drug deal?

Do you have a secret life moonlighting as a high-class escort?" Her eyes are wide and excited.

The trick to remembering your own lies is to keep them as close to the truth as possible.

I laugh. "Nothing so exciting. My aunt and uncle were in town. They left me a note at the front desk where"—I tilt my head in the direction Justin walked—"Justin works. My family always calls me Charlotte. It's after a great-great-grandparent or something."

"Oh. You didn't tell me you had family in town." She smacks my arm with the menu, though the hurt in her eyes makes the playful gesture more painful than it should be. "I would have loved to meet them."

Talk about a nightmare.

I suppress a cringe.

"They were just passing through. I missed them as well. Hence the note."

The waiter comes over to take our drink orders and as soon as he leaves, I change the subject to the mocktail night and Ben and anything else I can to distract her with until we leave the restaurant—and Justin—behind.

Tell the truth too long and you lose the knack of lying. Stay in one place too long, and those lies catch up with you. Maybe the parents are doing me a favor, showing up now and forcing us out. What ever made me think we could stop running from the truth?

We're walking off too many carne asada tacos down Main Street when Tabby stops and opens a shop door, motioning me to enter.

When I peer inside, it's a beauty salon.

"I made appointments to get our hair done."

"Tabby . . ."

"Before you argue, I already paid for it."

"Tabby . . ."

"Okay, I'm lying. I didn't pay for it. Jared did." She grins.

Dismay sinks into me. "He did?"

She laughs and nods, a whole lot more excited about that prospect than I am. "I told him where we were going and I might have mentioned getting our nails and hair done or something. Then he insisted it be his treat, since we're doing all this to help with the case, you know. Don't look so upset, Jared is totally loaded, he doesn't care. He also told me to tell you it's already been paid for, and if you back out, the money will be wasted. No refunds."

She pats me on the head and then walks into the salon.

I follow her.

The thing is . . . I do care.

Tabby makes me feel a little better, though. She gets super excited about getting our nails painted to match our dresses.

While our hands are drying, she asks, "What do you want to do to your hair?"

"I don't know." I shrug. "I guess cover up the roots or something."

She stops blowing on her nails and eyes me. "Why don't you go with your natural color? It looks like it's the same color as Paige's. She has beautiful hair. Why'd you dye it anyway?"

I shrug again. It was my mother. She insisted that blonds were better cons. Men love blonds, she would say. You have to use every advantage you can because you don't have many.

The last time I went to a salon, actually, was with my mother.

It was my twenty-first birthday and Mother took me to the spa—just me and her—for a girls' day.

To anyone on the outside, it was a great present, and we had a fabulous time. We drank champagne, got pedicures and facials. "You're so lucky," the manicurist said. "Your mother spoils you."

And she did, when people were there and watching and listening. She asked me questions and pretended like she cared. We'd played a game since I was a kid, one that sort of mimicked our reality. We would have conversations and pretend to be other people, making up stories as we went. When I was younger, it was little things, like I would tell her I won a spelling test, or she'd say she got a new job or a promotion. We would tell these stories to each other in front of people like they were real. We did it all the time. As I got older, the stories got more complicated and outrageous. The challenge was to keep all the details straight and natural sounding while Mom tried to trip me up in front of our audience. I got damn good at that game, despite the cantina catastrophe earlier.

We played the game that day at the spa. When Mom dropped the bomb that I was her daughter visiting from Harvard, I scrambled to remember anything I could use from *Good Will Hunting*. When the manicurist asked me what I was studying, I hesitated. What would I do, if I could do anything?

"Criminal justice," I told her.

Oh, to be on the right side of the law for once.

"I'm so proud of my daughter," Mother said. She smiled at me, and she made it look so real I almost believed it.

That was their gift, the parents. They could sell a gun to a pacifist. They were so convincing sometimes even I forgot they were the bad guys.

While we were driving home, Mother stopped. She pulled over on the side of the road and handed me a piece of paper.

It was a bank statement, one I had set up for me and Paige in our first attempt at an exit strategy. I had been slowly and carefully putting money into it for about six months. The printout she gave me showed a balance of three thousand dollars.

"Gone," she said, ripping up the page and throwing the pieces in my lap. "Don't try it again. I'll find it. And you know who's going to suffer? Paige."

We didn't speak the rest of the way home.

To prove her point, I didn't see Paige at all for a full week. They refused to tell me where she was.

When Paige came back home, I cried.

Paige, on the other hand, was perplexed.

They had sent her to a weeklong science camp at a nearby lake.

An oddity in and of itself. They barely ever let her leave the house.

I learned my lesson: They could take her away anytime they wanted. I had no power over them or what they did with her.

I still don't have power over the parents. No power over how long they will spend trying to find Paige and I, and no power over what they might do once they find us. But I do have power over myself. My choices. My actions. Right now. They can't take that away from me.

"Honey, what do you want to do with this mess?" My hairdresser is a dark-haired, thin man with bright eyes and flamboyant gestures. He picks up a limp blond strand, holding it between two fingers like it might bite him.

Our eyes connect in the mirror. "I want to go back to my natural color."

"Good idea." He nods, one finger pressed against his lips for a moment before he taps it. "Maybe a few subtle highlights." He bustles around me, murmuring, combing, and foiling and then washing and cutting. I try not to look as the dead strands of hair fall away.

Then he turns me away from the mirror. A blow dryer and circular brush emerge, and all I can hear is the hum of hot air as I'm fluffed and brushed within an inch of my life.

"Are you ready?" He purses his lips at me while still fluffing my hair.

I can see strands in my peripheral vision. No more bottled blond, it looks more like dark honey.

I swallow and nod. He spins me around.

It's me in the mirror. I know the face, the eyes, the button nose and too-full mouth. It's me. But it all appears drastically different underneath hair that's not mine. I mean, it's mine, I've just never seen it so . . . normal. So not like my mother.

"Dude. Jared is going to flip his shit." Tabby appears behind me in the mirror, her eyes wide, her mouth open. "You are a goddess. I mean, you've always been hot, but now you're like *hot* hot. Like, I will sleep with you if he doesn't."

I laugh, and the person in the mirror laughs too. It's so weird. What a difference a haircut makes.

19

———

We leave Roseburg after our hair is done and styled. Tabby has an updo with some dark strands of her hair pulled out, curling and framing her face. Mine is all down in waves that are somehow both sleek and bouncy. I don't know how hairdressers achieve what is nearly impossible for us mere mortals.

Tabby drops me off at Ruby's, where I'm meeting up with Paige before we head to Tabby's for dinner and to get ready for the night.

Paige oohs and ahhs over my new hairdo and dress. She's more excited than I am.

"Do you think if we weren't leaving, you would date Jared?"

I swallow, not realizing we had been so obvious. "I don't know, Paige. Even if we didn't have to leave tomorrow, Ruby is still coming back."

"What if it wasn't for that, either?"

I shrug. "Probably."

She frowns. "I'm sorry, Charlotte."

"It's not your fault."

I shrug off the depressing conversation and focus on the present. We drive over to Tabby's and make it there before five. Tabby has snacks and champagne at the ready, as well as a ton more makeup than I've ever owned in my whole life.

Even though I was initially reluctant to get all dolled up, I have to admit, it's kind of fun.

Paige sits on Tabby's bed and gives us pointers while she eats cheeseballs and drinks some sparkling cider that Tabby picked up for her. She poured the cider into a champagne glass so Paige isn't left out. I think what I love most about Tabby and Jared is how they've accepted both of us as a package deal. Because we are.

Tabby does my makeup, and she doesn't overdo it, thank god.

By the time I slip on some silver strappy heels, I feel like a princess.

"You guys look amazing," Paige says wistfully. "I wish I could go."

"You want to hang out with a bunch of old people that smell like Bengay and desperation?" Tabby asks.

Paige winces. "Maybe not."

"It's a school night, anyway."

Paige is staying at Naomi's and taking the bus with her the next day to school. The last day of school.

We meet each other's eyes in the mirror, and I know we're thinking the same thing.

I shrug the thoughts away. Have to focus.

"You all packed up?" Tabby asks Paige.

She is, and we pile into Tabby's car. We drop Paige off at Naomi's and then make our way to the senior center.

Jared and Troy should already be here. They planned to arrive before the first guests so that they would be on hand and available to observe the arrivals.

The cafeteria at the senior center has been transformed into something resembling a middle-school dance. The lights are dim, streamers hang limply from the ceiling, and a disco ball slowly rotates in the center. In one corner is a DJ set up on a narrow stage. "The Lady in Red" croons from the speakers.

There are couples all over the dance floor. It's a sea of colorful sequins and shoulder pads with the occasional dark suit.

I think I catch a flash of dark hair somewhere in the mix of grays—must be Troy or Jared.

Ben is off toward the corner of the room opposite the DJ, behind a long table that's substituting as a bar. I spy Miss Viola "sleeping" in her wheelchair near him. Her purple sequined dress flashes under the spinning lights.

Tabby and I head in Ben's direction since that's her station for the night.

"You guys want a drink? I've got cranberry fizzies." Ben says "cranberry fizzies" like we're toddlers and he's trying to entice us to eat our leafy greens. He's teasing, but underneath his words there's an undercurrent of strain, like he's putting on a not-very-convincing act.

"So tempting." Tabby grimaces.

Ben nods at her and sets down a drink in front of her.

She eyes it for a few long seconds, like she might not drink it at all, but then she takes a small sip. "Ugh. Club soda. This is so depressing."

"Thanks," Ben deadpans.

I haven't seen them together since Tabby told me about the whole no-more-making-out thing, and I can sense some tension here, despite my conversational beating of Ben.

I smile at Ben and thank him when he hands me a cranberry mocktini. "I'm gonna go mingle. Let me know if you see anything."

I run into Judge and Mrs. Ramsey and stop to say hi and shake hands.

While talking to them, I spot Mrs. Olsen. She somehow found a bright red dress with a purple sequined cat on the butt.

Dear lord.

And then I see Jared. He's dancing with Mrs. Hale, holding her hand, his arm around her back, waltzing her gently around the dance floor.

He's wearing a black and white tux that fits his broad shoulders perfectly and tapers down to his slim waist.

His dark-blue eyes slide over me and then double back as recognition lights over his features.

I stop breathing.

His smile is devastation to my sheltered heart.

Dancers move in between us, blocking him from view. When we lose eye contact, I can breathe again. But not for long. When the path between us clears, I try to find him and Mrs. Hale, but they've disappeared.

I glance around the room, eventually spotting Mrs. Hale talking to Mr. Godfrey over at the bar, but Jared isn't with them.

"Hey," a voice says in my ear.

I jump. "What the hell, Jared? Where did you come from?"

"I've got ninja moves." He smirks. "You look . . . amazing." His eyes trail from my face down and then back up.

"You don't look so bad yourself."

The tux is even better up close.

I want to climb him like a jungle gym.

"Here." From behind his back he pulls out a flower in a plastic case.

"What is this?" My heart is thumping so loudly I'm surprised he can't hear it.

"What do you think?"

It's a light-blue flower surrounded by tufts of baby's breath. It matches my dress.

I think I stop breathing.

"Tabby said something about you never going to prom," Jared says. "So I thought I could, I don't know, make up for it or something."

He sounds nervous.

Probably because I'm still standing here, gaping at him like I'm trying to catch food in my mouth and he's throwing it. I force myself to breathe and shut my lips together.

I'll never have this opportunity again, and goddammit I'm going to enjoy it.

I take the box and open it, pulling out the flowers. There's an elastic tie attached to the back.

"Thank you." I'm literally blinking away tears.

Dear lord, get a grip on yourself, woman. You're a con artist, not a crybaby.

A lump forms in my throat. I am just a con. And this shouldn't mean anything.

But it does.

He helps me put the flower on my wrist, then he sets the plastic box on a nearby table.

"Have you seen—" I start.

"What do you—" he says at the same time.

We laugh and I have to avert my eyes from his.

"You go first." He takes my hand without the flower on it and tucks it in his arm while we walk around the edge of the room.

"Have you seen anything worth mentioning?"

"Not yet. We couldn't exactly do a pat down of all of these people, but Troy has been checking purses in the coatroom for extra keys. What about you? Have you gotten any strange vibes?"

He gazes down at me and I get lost in his dark eyes for a minute.

"No," I say. "But the night is young."

Jared has the list of suspects in his pocket, but he doesn't need it. He murmurs their names to me as we circle around the room. We stop to talk to people occasionally, but everyone seems normal and completely sober and no one gives off any breaking-and-entering vibes. Eventually, we end up at the bar, where Tabby is still giving Ben the occasional evil eye.

"Anything?" Jared asks them.

Tabby shrugs and Ben shakes his head.

"Nothing," he says. "They aren't even trying to steal the maraschino cherries like they normally do. It's like they're behaving themselves extra because you guys are here. Maybe you should have hidden or something."

Jared shakes his head. "Well, if they're all behaving we might as well enjoy ourselves. Would you like to dance?"

"I can't dance," I say.

"You couldn't swim either." He's smiling at me, eyes twinkling.

"Go dance." Tabby smacks me on the arm. "Look," she points, "Mrs. Seinfeld is out there with a walker. No excuses. You don't have to know how to do anything, you just hang on for the ride."

And then it's like I'm starring in one of those cheeseball eighties teen movies because the song switches to "Time After Time" and Jared takes my hand and leads me to the dance floor, winding through the other slow-moving dancers.

"What is it with this music?"

"It's an eighties theme tonight. I guess they've been going through the decades since this whole thing started."

"Oh." I have no idea what else to say. I can't speak over the flutters in my stomach.

Jared puts one hand on my back and the other grips my hand.

My skin prickles with awareness everywhere he touches, sending electric currents straight to my stomach. I don't know whether to run away or jump him.

"Are you ready?"

Absolutely not. But I nod anyway.

He moves slowly. It's not like we can swing around, surrounded by the blue-hairs in all their sequined, shuffling, glory. The disco ball flashes, casting colorful lights all around. It's sort of magical, even when I nearly trip over Mrs. Seinfeld's walker and Jared has to catch me.

The heat of his hand on my back is both soothing and tormenting. It's almost too romantic and I have to remind myself why I'm here in the first place.

"What's the plan for the rest of the night?" I glance around. "We know our perp has got to be here somewhere. How are we going to catch them?"

"Anderson is parked down the road a ways. He's going to try and trail people as they leave." His hand tightens on my waist. "I almost don't want to find the Castle Cove ghost."

"Why not?"

"Because then I won't have any excuse to keep you."

Startled, I meet his gaze.

His eyes are intent and serious.

"I . . ."

"I know this scares you." The words are gravelly and serious. "I know you aren't ready for me. For this. But I'm not giving up. We have something here. I won't push you, but I will wait for you."

I'm speechless. Within forty-eight hours, I'll be gone forever. I can't lead him on, I can't make him think this could be something when it could never be anything.

The dancers around us become a blur.

"Jared, I like you. A lot." Probably the most honest statement I've made since we met. "And I cannot tell you how much you mean to me, and to Paige, too. And that's why I don't want to lead you on."

I expect him to get upset or angry, but instead he grins at me like I just said I want to make out with him.

"Why are you smiling?"

He shrugs. "You said you like me. I'm taking that as progress. You're telling me there's a chance."

A surprised laugh bursts out of me.

"Hey." Troy comes up next to us, placing a hand on Jared's shoulder. "Sorry to interrupt the schmoozing, but we have an issue."

"What is it?"

"Tabby said Mrs. Olsen is drunk."

"How is that possible? Ben and I tested all the drinks and we checked all the purses for booze."

"Well, I'm not sure. But she's making out with Mr. Godfrey in the coat closet, so we could check in there again."

We're no longer dancing, but Jared has my hand in his. He squeezes it once before releasing me.

"I'll go check in with Tabby," I say.

They head off toward the coatroom.

Still standing on the dance floor, I glance over at the bar, intending on heading in that direction.

Tabby and Ben appear to be actually talking instead of fighting. I don't want to interrupt them if they're making some kind of progress.

Maybe Ben actually listened to me. Maybe they'll find happiness when I'm gone.

Maybe Jared will, too.

With someone who's not me.

The fluttering in my stomach turns sour.

I need some air.

20

The night breeze strokes my face with cool, salty air as I make my way through the parking lot. There's an overlook with a small bench facing the ocean. I sit, gazing out over the dark water. The contrast of the bright moon against the dark sky sprinkled with stars soothes my weary mind.

A shooting star flashes across the sky and I let out a gasp.

I've never seen one before. I've never been a big believer in magic, or fate, or any of the lines I've been selling, but in this moment, I want to.

I shut my eyes and make a wish. I wish I could stay. I wish I could have this life that I've taken over for the last two months. I wish I were stronger.

Too many wishes probably negates the whole thing. I open my eyes and spy a small gap in the wood fence in front of me. It's the entrance to a narrow, sandy path that leads down toward the beach. I follow the curve with my eyes. The beach leads over to the bluffs where the castle is.

Something glints in the moonlight. Something shiny. I stare at it in the darkness, leaning forward, craning my neck like it will help me see better. It doesn't really, but the shape does start to make more sense. It looks like . . . a chair.

Wait. Not just any chair. A wheelchair.

"Holy shit."

It's got to be Miss Viola's wheelchair. I frantically think back to the last time I saw her. She was sleeping over by the bar. When I checked on Ben and Tabby before I left the building, I didn't see her.

I know she's not as deaf as she pretends, but could she be pretending to need the chair as well?

Her name was on the list both Ben and Mr. Bingel gave us. Both lists. But I never would have even considered her because she can't walk.

Or can she?

My eyes are drawn back up to the moon.

Full.

I remember what Jared said, what Mr. Bingel confirmed. Walking the plank naked under the full moon.

She's doing it tonight. Now.

I squint into the darkness, trying to see anything moving on the grassy hill in the distance. Under the light of the moon, something shimmers. The dark purple shimmer of a sequined dress. Miss Viola.

I have to stop her. Even if she's more agile than I realized, she's going to get herself killed.

No time to go back to the senior center for help, I scramble off the bench and then down the sandy path after her, toward the bluffs.

"Damn that old lady," I mutter, air wheezing in and out of my lungs as I run as fast as I can through the sand. My shoes aren't helping. Irritated, I pull them off and leave them on the beach. I continue running toward the path leading up to the castle, the same one the Newsomes used for their skinny-dipping adventure.

By the time I reach the stairs, I'm winded and my calves are burning. I really need to work out more.

I push myself up the hill toward the castle. I pass by a crumbling bit of giant rock where a purple sequined dress hangs from a jagged protrusion.

Oh, no. I run faster, urging my tired muscles on. When I reach the top of the hill, near the precipice, I see her. She's wearing a thin white slip. It falls to her knees, the fabric fluttering in the breeze. She looks no bigger than Paige up there on the broad wooden post that spans what remains of the two large towers. And she hasn't started walking the plank yet; she's still hovering at the edge, her back against the rock wall.

"Miss Viola!" I call, scrambling up the hill toward the bottom of the closest hunk of rock.

My voice catches on the wind and gets thrown back in my face.

If her hearing is anywhere near as bad as she lets on,

there's no way she's going to be able to hear me. I've got to go after her.

When I reach the bottom of the boulder, I find a series of embedded footholds and wooden grips wedged into the rocks. How the hell did the old lady get up this thing?

Well. There's nothing for it. I allow myself a few deep breaths, and then I haul myself up toward the plank.

"Miss Viola, don't move!" I call out. I can't see her, but hopefully she's still standing near where I'll be coming up. The last section is the hardest. My already tired muscles are screaming at me as I pull myself up and onto the ledge. The tearing sound of my dress ripping up the side adds a nice little middle finger to my night.

Dammit. Now I won't be able to return it.

"Miss Viola, thank god!"

She's only a couple feet away, just beginning her walk. The wooden board is about three feet wide. There are spots that appear thinner and narrower—and more dangerous—the farther it goes.

"You can't stop me," she says when she sees me. "They stopped me once before, but this time I'm going to finish this."

"Miss Viola, it's not safe."

"I don't care. I hear them talking even though they think I don't. They still talk about the glory days and how they all got to be in that club. I was invited too, you know, but then the last night of the initiation, we got busted up here and since I never finished, I never got to be a part of it. Well, now that time is over, my little piddle pie."

Piddle pie?

"Now they're trying to outdo me. *I* started up the old tradition. *I* did all the steps again from beginning to end. And now *I* am going to be the first initiate in decades. I'm not gonna let them horn in on it and one-up me."

So on top of surprising athleticism, Miss Viola has developed a streak of paranoia too? "No one's trying to one-up you."

"Don't try to hoodwink me, child. They're trying to steal my thunder!"

This is the most I've ever heard Miss Viola speak without yelling or saying something wildly inappropriate. She looks almost like a ghost up here in the wind, her short white hair fluttering in the breeze with her slip, and she's not blinking, like at all.

It's kinda creepy.

"Ruby!" Jared's voice echoes over the cliffs from the beach access.

The cavalry has arrived. Jared and Troy are flying up the path, Tabby behind them.

"Dammit," Miss Viola curses. "Not again."

She starts shuffling faster across the board but falters when she trips over a nail.

"No!" I yell.

She manages to straighten herself a bit before turning toward me, her hands on her hips, her face defiant. "I'm finishing this no matter what, missy."

"At least . . . let me help you." She's unsteady, and it's more than just the ocean breeze. Who knows how long she's been sitting in that damn wheelchair unnecessarily, but I know my limbs are sore from the run through the beach and the climb, and even if Miss Viola went much slower than me, she's got to be tired.

I creep out from my post near the tower where I've been gripping the rocks behind me and inch closer to her.

"I can do this on my own." She shuffles a few steps away.

"But I can help you."

"Back off, hussy!"

"Miss Viola!" If I weren't afraid of one or the both of us tumbling into the dark, churning water below, I might be laughing right now.

"Ruby, hang on! We're coming!" Tabby's voice is loud and panicked.

They're getting closer.

Which is making Miss Viola move even faster.

Willing myself not to look down, I follow her.

I've almost reached her when Tabby starts yelling again.

"Oh my god, Ruby, don't die!"

I roll my eyes.

"Stop being so dramatic," Miss Viola calls back down to her, reading my thoughts.

But when Miss Viola waves her hands in the direction of the others, she loses her footing again and starts to tip.

"No!" My voice a near whisper, I reach for her.

I clasp her arm in mine and we wobble for a moment, teetering on the edge of the creaking board.

I plant my feet and bend my knees for stability. It takes a few long seconds, but I finally set us aright and let out a shaky laugh when we're both standing securely.

"That was close," Miss Viola says.

Then her eyes roll back in her head and she slouches against me.

Oh, shit. She's fainted. I can't hold on to her. She's small but heavier than I expected. I tilt to the side.

We're going to fall. I can't avoid it, so I have to make a decision. There are only two directions to go, one is down onto the grassy embankment, and while that seems like it would be better than falling off the cliff, it's hard and unyielding earth. One of us, at the very least, might not survive. Our other option is the churning black water. It's not too far, really, maybe forty feet, like Jared told me once before.

He said when the tide was high it would be safe.

The board cracks underneath our combined weight. I pray to whoever is out there that the water is deep enough.

Then I throw our weight toward the cliff.

Someone's yelling, but all I can hear is the wind in my ears as Miss Viola and I fall down the bluffs and into the freezing water.

21

So the ocean is nothing like the pool.

My body gets a shocking jolt from the frigid water, forcing the air from my lungs.

I know nothing but cold and darkness and then my brain remembers swimming and my legs start kicking. I find myself above the churning waves, but Miss Viola is gone.

Dammit.

I flap around, getting hit in the face with water while trying to feel for Miss Viola.

"Miss Viola," I gasp. "Miss Viola!"

"I've got you, child." The voice is in my ear right as an arm comes around my neck. "Lay still." She pulls me backward in the water.

Is she towing me to shore?

"Miss V, I can swim." I pull away, but she's strong for an old tiny lady and I end up swallowing a mouth full of salt water.

"It's okay. Just lie back and let it happen," she says.

Oh dear lord.

Then there's a loud splash behind us and a yell.

"Ruby!"

It's Jared.

He jumped in after us.

"Over here," I call, still trying to escape from Miss Viola's clutches.

Her fingers are like talons on my shoulder.

A couple of strokes and he's there, water churning between us as we sway in the waves. In the brightness of the moon I can see his eyes, wide and worried.

"Are you all right?"

Miss Viola answers before I can. "I'm fine. Thanks for asking, Deputy."

We ignore her.

"You jumped in after us," I say.

"You're okay," he says, like he's just now realizing that even though he's been staring straight at me for the last twenty seconds.

"Why did you jump? What if it had been low tide?"

He doesn't answer. His eyes are locked on me as he paddles less than a foot away.

"I'm swimming in. It's cold out here, and I think you can take this one from here," Miss Viola says.

She releases her hold around my neck and then she's splashing away.

I don't watch her, though. All I care about is the man in front of me. The man who jumped off a cliff after me.

I grab his face and kiss him, hard. The motion causes

us both to slip underwater for a moment before Jared kicks us back up to the surface.

"Sorry."

"Don't be." He grabs my arms and wraps them around his neck. "Hold that thought though, okay?" He pulls me onto his back and we follow Miss Viola back to the shore.

The beach is crowded with elderly people in fancy clothes.

There's an ambulance and a fire truck, and even the mayor stopped by to hear the story.

Excitement like this doesn't happen often in Castle Cove.

Miss V soaks it all in, gleefully embellishing the story and laughing about snowing all of us for so long. Mrs. Olsen is hurt, though. She really thought Miss V was her friend—even though she basically used her friend as a shopping cart every time they hung out—and can't believe Miss Viola lied to her this whole time.

Once the EMT clears me of any injuries or hypothermia and Anderson takes my statement, I get to leave.

Jared wants to bring me back to his house, but I convince him to take me home. To Ruby's.

I can't keep living the lie. We have to prepare for tomorrow night and I can't do that from Jared's.

I'm glad that the mystery is solved and everyone is

okay, but I'm worn out as all hell. I shower and fall into bed as the sun is coming up.

I sleep until noon, when Paige finally comes home and wakes me.

She's heard all about my little dive off the bluffs, but I give her the firsthand version over eggs and pancakes.

Then we go over everything, one last time.

Her bag is already at the school, in her locker.

Naomi's grandma is dropping them off at the dance.

The rest of the day is relatively quiet. I expected our last day in Castle Cove to be more . . . climactic.

Tabby stops by to check on me. She's going on a date, an actual date with Ben. Apparently, he listened to my advice and wants to take her out somewhere special. He asked her out right before Jared realized I was missing, which made them realize Miss Viola was also missing and they came looking for us.

I'm happy. She's happy. She deserves every bit of joy she can wring from this life, even if I won't be around to witness it.

I wait for Jared to call or stop by. He doesn't. I shouldn't be bothered. It's going to be hard enough to leave without having to see him one last time.

Paige leaves for Naomi's after dinner and I'm home alone.

I set my alarm for nine, figuring I should try and nap. I need to get some sleep, knowing tonight will be a long night of driving.

But I can't sleep.

I can't stop thinking about everything. What if our

parents still find us? What if the new car breaks down before we make it somewhere? What if, what if . . .

Judge Ramsey and his words about life run through my head.

I think about Jared's lips on mine, the heat a contrast to the cold, salty ocean.

I'm never going to see him again.

At seven, I finally give up and get out of bed. If I were someone else, I would be on my date with Jared right now, but I blew him off. It's for the best, but . . .

Going to him now, before I leave . . . it would be both amazing and destructive.

I still have plenty of time until I have to meet Paige, and I have to see him, one more time. Even if it ends up hurting me more in the long run. I deserve the pain.

My feet have a mind of their own. Not caring that I'm dressed in plain cotton PJ shorts and a tank top, I leave the house with our small bags and walk to the mechanic's shop.

It's part of our plan, anyway. I'm supposed to pick up the car before meeting Paige at the rendezvous point. I'm just picking it up a little early.

It doesn't take long to get to the car. It's where the mechanic told me he would leave it, in the back, unlocked, the keys stashed in an envelope under the seat.

It turns over on the first try.

The car practically steers itself to Jared's house.

I park behind the Jeep in the circular driveway and

sit in the car for a few minutes. What the hell am I doing?

The lights are on inside, the soft glow beckoning me out of the car.

I jog up to the front door and knock gently.

The thudding of my heart in my ears is almost deafening.

What if he doesn't answer?

What if he answers and then sends me away?

What if—

The door opens.

His hair is mussed, but his eyes are alert.

"Ruby," he says.

I don't want to hear him say that name, so I kiss him.

It's not the most graceful of attempts. I step forward through the doorway and press my mouth against his, but I miss and catch the corner of his mouth. I pull back to correct the error, but before I can zero in on my target, he grabs my head and his lips crash into mine.

The tension in my body drains away as the heat in my stomach builds and spreads.

My hands run up, underneath his shirt, over the ridges of his stomach, pulling the fabric up and over his head before moving in to kiss him some more.

I can't get enough. I want him everywhere. Over me, under me, around me . . . in me. Now.

His hands run down by back, warm and needy—mimicking my own thoughts—too much, not enough, he cups my rear in his hands, flexing and pulling me closer against him. Then we're stumbling inside.

The door slams behind me and then he pushes me against it, his hands moving under the thin fabric of my top and yanking it over my head before we come together again. Mouths, tongues, hands everywhere. I can't stop. I don't want to stop. It's the last time I'll ever see him, and I need to make it count.

When my fingers start tugging the elastic band of his shorts, he pulls back and peers into my eyes.

"Are you sure?" The entryway is dark and his voice is deep and rough.

"Yes." Is that me speaking, all breathy and low?

"It's just, you've been pushing me away and—"

"Jared," I say, my voice a little louder, "I'm sure. I've never been so sure of anything in my life. Now, less talking, more kissing."

"Yes ma'am." And then we don't speak again. At least, not with words. His hands are reverent on me, gentle and searching. His shorts stay on, for now, while we tease and kiss in the foyer.

My body is heating while my heart is breaking. This is it. The last time I'll see Jared, the last opportunity I'll have to be with him. I'm grateful for knowing him and devastated all at once. I know he has to see my emotions in my eyes, sense it in my touch, because he groans and then moves his mouth to my neck and then lower. His finger slides under the collar of my tank top, pulling it down, exposing my breasts to both the stinging cool of the night air and the heat of his breath.

His lips meander farther downward, until he's kneeling in front of me. His palms skim up my legs, gently sliding my shorts off and away and then his mouth covers me through the thin barrier of my cotton panties.

"Oh my god," I gasp, my head falling back against the door.

The heat of his mouth on my most intimate place and the scratch of his stubble on my thighs nearly ends me right there, against the door.

I've never done this, never felt this, never want to feel it with anyone else, ever.

"Jared," I moan when he pushes the fabric aside and slowly slides a finger inside me.

Between the glide of his lips and the pressure of his finger, I can't possibly take any more without spontaneously combusting. Right before I explode, he stops.

"What are you doing?"

"We're going to do this right." He stands and picks me up, carrying me down the hallway toward his bedroom.

22

———

I alternate watching the clock and watching Jared sleep. He's on his stomach, naked, a sheet covering him up to the waist. My eyes trail over the muscles of his back and shoulders and settle on his face.

He's so beautiful, outside and in. I can't deny the heat his body ignites inside me, but it's more than that. He cares about people. He gives without expecting anything in return. It's like I've found a unicorn in a forest full of trolls, and now I have to leave him behind.

I gaze at him as long as I can, long enough to take the memory with me.

When I can't possibly push it any longer, I get out of bed and get dressed. My clothes are strewn between the bedroom and the front door, and I pick the items up as I move through the house.

In the kitchen, I hesitate when I spot a pad of paper on the counter next to a pen.

I scrawl a quick message.

Gravy jumps up on the counter and sprawls down in front of my note, his torn ear twitching in my direction while his luminous eyes watch me.

He's not hissing.

Why isn't he hissing? He always either attacks or shrieks. There's never anything in between.

He ducks his head, resting it on his outstretched paws, then he purrs—a few brief beats.

It's like he's saying goodbye.

My eyes water.

I will not cry over the damn devil cat.

As if he can read my mind, he swats me with a paw—claws retracted—and leaps off the counter, disappearing down the hall, tail flicking pretentiously behind him.

I sigh. Jared will take good care of him.

He'll find my note. He'll be a little confused about a seemingly unprompted apology. But then he'll call the shop, or stop by, and I won't be there. He'll talk to Tabby and find out we left Gravy and then . . . the real Ruby will eventually return. Will he hate me? Will the lies taint the truth that lived between us?

Time is running out. It's nearly ten.

I have to get Paige.

With one last glance around, I sneak out the front door, but I don't make it to the car.

"Paige?" I'm frozen in the doorway.

She's here. But she's not supposed to be here, she's supposed to be at the rendezvous point. My brain stutters to a stop, failing to work through the implications, but my wicked, traitorous eyes keep going, taking in every detail and presenting the scene to me with malicious glee.

She's standing at the bottom of the short flight of steps that leads to the gravel drive, illuminated by the porch lights. She's still in her new dress. Her eyes are red and mascara streaks down her face like charcoal tears.

And she's not alone.

"You can have her back as soon as you fix our little problem." Red-tipped nails grip Paige's shoulder like talons. It's a voice I recognize. A voice I've gone to great pains to never hear again.

Shock pulses through me.

They're here.

At Jared's.

He's sleeping peacefully less than a hundred feet away.

Then Mother explains, "You see, you stole a bit of money from us and now you're going to pay it back. With interest."

Not quite the end . . .

The third and final book in the Castle Cove Mystery Series is now available! Find You're the Con That I Want today at your preferred retailer!

ABOUT THE AUTHOR

Go here to sign up for the newsletter!
www.authormaryframe.com

Mary Frame is a full-time mother and wife with a full-time job. She has no idea how she manages to write novels except that it helps being a dedicated introvert. She doesn't enjoy writing about herself in third person, but she does enjoy reading, writing, dancing, and damaging the eardrums of her coworkers when she randomly decides to sing to them. She lives in Reno, Nevada, with her husband, two children, and a border collie named Stella.

She LOVES hearing from readers and will not only respond but likely begin stalking them while tossing out hearts and flowers and rainbows! If that doesn't creep you out, email her at: maryframeauthor@gmail.com
Follow her on Twitter: @marewulf
Like her Facebook author page: www.facebook.com/AuthorMaryFrame

Imperfect Series reading order:
Book One: Imperfect Chemistry

Book Two: Imperfectly Criminal
Book Three: Practically Imperfect
Book Four: Picture Imperfect
Book Five: Imperfect Strangers
Book Six: Imperfectly Delicious

Looking for more nerdy romance?
Check out this dorky spin-off duet!
The Dorky Duet (Plus a companion novel!)
Rirdorkulous
Geektastic
Nerdelicious

The Extraordinary Series
Anything But Extraordinary
A Life Less Extraordinary
Extraordinary World

Time After Time Series:
Time of My Life
If I Could Turn Back Time

Fox Family Series
Between a Fox and a Hard Place
The Fox and the Rebound